Insurrection

The Machine: Book Two

Philip N. Rogone

This is a work of fiction. The names, characters, places, and incidents are the product of the author's imagination or are used fictitiously. Any resemblance to actual events, locales, or persons, living or dead, is entirely coincidental and only meant for dramatic effect.

ISBNs

eBook: 979-8-9942482-1-8
Paperback: 97809864209-0-0
Hardcover: 978-0-9864209-7-9

Contents

This book is dedicated to my heroes.

My brothers

***Cpl. John Pio Rogone,** USMC, Forest Recon, killed in action, Quan Tri Province, Viet Nam, June 29th, 1968.*

***Sgt. Peter Anthony Rogone,** U.S. Army 101st Airborne Division, Black Beret Tunnel Rat in Viet Nam, and Purple Heart recipient.*

And especially my father, Staff Sgt. **Philip N. Rogone Sr.,** *U.S. Army World War II BAR Man, Veteran, and Purple Heart recipient who was wounded multiple times from Africa to Italy under General Patton.*

There is no longer any room for hope. If we wish to be free—if we mean to preserve inviolate those inestimable privileges for which we have been so long contending—if we mean not basely to abandon the noble struggle in which we have been so long engaged, and which we have pledged ourselves never to abandon until the glorious object of our contest shall be obtained—we must fight! I repeat it, sir, we must fight! An appeal to arms and to the God of hosts is all that is left to us!

Patrick Henry, March 23, 1775

The maxim of Jefferson, "equal rights to all and special privileges to none," and the doctrine of Lincoln that this should be a government "of the people, by the people and for the people," are being disregarded and the instrumentalities of government are being used to advance the interests of those who are in a position to secure favors from the Government.

William Jennings Bryant August 8, 1900

There is a poison infiltrating my country, and those in charge have become so corrupt and politically correct, they have turned a blind eye to this internal attack. I'm afraid some of those elected by the people have, in fact, become the enemy. They are holding tight to their position solely for the sake of re-election and the power it brings. This leaves me with no choice but to fight. If I find an American politician or his minion working to hurt America, I'll dissect him and leave his miserable carcass on the steps of the Capitol.

Secret Service Agent Michael Angelino

From his journal, December 2002

Prologue

Tess Lamia sat quietly in her new boss's office as he reviewed the carnage that took place in the Philippines. Ted Hobson began reading the gruesome details of an entire Jihadist camp decimated by long-distance sniper fire and close kills by stabbing with a blade of unrecognized configuration, all the while watching his assistant for a reaction. She listened nervously as he continued.

"Michael Angelino is a killing machine, and he appears to be out of control. My God, the dentist strapped in his chair, fingers cut off with what appears to be a hunting knife, and his head severed and placed in his own lap. The forensic team said that based on the blood splatter, Michael was nose to nose with him when he decapitated the guy."

"Let's not forget, Ted, that this dentist you're talking about was possibly part of a Jihadist hit squad planning to kill the President, blow up Galveston Bay, and oh yeah, kill most of the people in Los Angeles, including most of the Governors of the United States. Do you really think an aging FBI agent ready for retirement could do what you're suggesting?"

"Yes, I do, Tess." Ted calmly responded.

Tess continued. "Michael Angelino on his best day couldn't accomplish that kind of carnage. Who do you think he is, Superman? I've worked with him for over ten years, and it's just not in his nature." Tess concluded with firm conviction.

"Really? Let's look at your friend's nature, shall we?" Ted said as he opened a file with Michael's name on it. "It seems your dear friend loves knives, and they have documented over a hundred kills without firing a weapon. Reports were filed by soldiers in and around Huang Tri Province of finding the carcasses of skinned human beings hanging from trees or on the ground with their hearts excised or other parts inserted into places I won't even mention. Who the hell do you think did this carnage, Tess, the boogie man?" Ted slammed the file on the desk and approached his beautiful assistant. "Tess, he may have been the nicest man in the world, but when he hit his head on 9/11, it unleashed a killing machine, and this guy isn't taking prisoners."

Tess sat there, tears slowly finding their way down her cheeks. She grabbed a tissue as her boss continued.

"The reason I need you to get these facts into your head is so we can help the poor bastard."

Tess looked at her boss in disbelief as he continued talking. "We need to work together to find a way to provide him with information about other cells. Let's face it, they're sure to be activated because of the butchery done to their comrades, and we can assume they're aware of that fact as we speak." Ted looked at her intently and continued. "It's my guess if he trusts anyone, it would be you, Tess."

"What do you want me to do, Ted?" she asked, still untrusting of his intentions.

"I believe it will only be a matter of time before he contacts you. Let him know we will be providing him with whatever information might help him in his fight. We will, however, deny any knowledge of his actions, and he will ultimately be alone. This is, unfortunately, the exact position Michael was in back in Nam. Letting him loose but denying any knowledge of his existence. The only good news for him is that he understands the game."

In Mexico City, the police were still trying to piece together the attack at one of their city's best five-star hotels. The crime scene was a bloodied mess. The eyewitnesses indicated some type of military attack and described the assailants dressed all in black. Their already over-crowded morgue was holding twenty-one new bodies, and the forensic doctor was trying to get identification from fingerprints.

The drug cartel denied any involvement, which meant that perhaps some other group had attacked the Middle Eastern businessman and his entourage. Calls from the office of the President of Mexico to the State Department were harshly accusing the United States of disregarding the borders of their country. U. S. officials from the State Department were sent out to investigate any government organization that might have crossed over into Mexico. The response from each agency was "we have no knowledge of any American involvement that took place within the sovereign borders of Mexico." The Mexican government wasn't buying that answer for a minute and made it clear in their correspondence with the President.

Detective Gil Astric was still swearing under his breath at the carnage in the San Bernardino strip joint, and the complete uselessness of the eyewitness reports that were all so different he could not substantiate any of the facts. The only thing he knew for sure was that this attacker killed a lot of men in a crowded place without injuring any innocents. The call he received from the killer was bothering him because his gut told him that he was one of the good guys, but his job was to find him and put his ass in jail. The local FBI confirmed that this was a group of Middle Eastern jihadists who were on a mission to attack the Governor's conference in Los Angeles. Astric didn't get a chance to interrogate the only survivor of the group because he was whisked away to Guantanamo

Bay Detention Camp in Cuba. However, Astric had gleaned enough information to know with relative certainty that the unknown killer probably saved the entire West Coast.

The confrontation that took place at the Badian Resort in the Philippines left all the signs of a full-blown combat zone. The vacation spot was littered with bodies shot, slashed, or blown up, and buildings destroyed by high-powered military hardware. There was only one survivor found on the beach, who was questioned by interrogators. All Honesto Fedorka could tell the authorities was that the man who attacked him by the water's edge said his sister sent him, but before he could react, he was knocked out. They brought Alice Fedorka in for questioning, but all she could tell them was that the man's name was John Doe and he was looking for a very bad man by the name of Zafeer El-Amin. She knew a bit more about him, but decided to keep it to herself out of gratitude for keeping her brother safe.

The second location in the jungles of Mindanao was so horrific that it frightened the Philippine military general who was brought in to investigate. His men found no survivors. Many of the victims had their throats cut or puncture wounds around the neck and groin area. Many others had large holes in their head from what appeared to be a high-powered rifle. The officer in charge indicated in his official report that a force of unknown size had killed ninety-three men in and around the camp. He privately told his staff that they should throw a parade for whoever did this, because it was one less group of jihadists to deal with. They found and identified Zafeer El-Amin on the top of a hill overlooking the campsite. He had a single shot to the head right between his eyes. The Associated Press put a photo of Zafeer in their article about the attack on the Muslim extremist group, and within minutes, those who had sent Zafeer became aware of his fate.

Michael Angelino stood in front of the bathroom sink and rinsed off the excess shaving cream from his head and ears. His goatee was now dark brown, and his head was totally bald. He took a long look at himself as he reviewed what had become of his life.

After receiving a concussion on 9/11 in the Pentagon, Michael began having blackouts. During these episodes, Michael resurrected a part of himself dubbed by his peers in Vietnam as The Machine. A black ops operative was given the assignment to kill in any way he saw fit. This part of himself lost its humanity in the jungles of Southeast Asia. He did not just kill his targets, but when time permitted, he would dissect them or skin them, all to psychologically affect the enemy. His kills numbered over 250, and many were killed at very close quarters without the use of a high-powered rifle or even a revolver. Instead, the soldier's weapon of choice was a homemade blade he nicknamed Betty. That tool of his trade was used to puncture the skin and lacerate essential arteries in the neck and the groin because they were larger vessels and would render the enemy helpless in a matter of seconds. This was the monster part of himself he tried to bury forever. The blackout disorder caused by the head injury continued during his beloved wife, Elle's, fight with cancer and after her death as well.

Tess Lamia, a woman who worked with and admired Michael for over ten years, confessed her love for him some time after his wife's death, but he was so depressed about her passing that going home to his empty house was too much for him. He told Tess he also had feelings for her, but needed to get away from the home in Gettysburg he shared with Elle for twenty years.

At a friend's request, he agreed to take a job with the Secret Service as part of the President's advance team. After his training at the James J Rowley Training Center (JJRT) near Washington, DC., he was given an assignment in Galveston, Texas. At their last dinner together, Michael confessed to her that he also had feelings for Tess, and the dinner ended with a kiss that stirred his emotions and a bit of guilt.

Once he arrived in Galveston, the two agents decided to split their assignment based on their area of expertise, with Michael taking potential terrorist threats. It was there that he met Brittany Abbey, a young woman trying to restart her life. They had become fast friends, and Michael saw her as a potential girlfriend for his very busy son Joshua.

When going to meet Brittany after her shift at the restaurant, she was shot by someone in a fast-moving black sedan. Michael blacked out, and when he recovered, he found himself in the recovery room talking with FBI agents he had summoned to the hospital to have her removed to a safe location.

Once he left the hospital, he blacked out again. Michael found those who had fired on Britt and discovered they were part of an activated terrorist cell. During that last blackout, Michael tracked down each and then one by one killed them all in one horrible twelve-hour period. When he recovered from the blackout, everything he had done during it came to the surface. The monster he had become some thirty-two years before was now resurrected forever.

THE MACHINE, a killing force of one, was known by the enemy as Doctor Fo (mad doctor) because of the horrifying body mutilations he left in his wake. They would run in terror upon discovering one of their own in pieces. Most often, they would find the heart of the man removed and placed in one of the outstretched hands.

Upon leaving the jungles of Vietnam, he vowed to devote his life to God and his family. He had all but forgotten the monster in the jungles, but the blackouts had resurrected him, and it was that part of him who began to do what he was an expert at, and that was killing. First, he did a reconnaissance of the enemy, then determined their force size, discovered a pattern in their everyday life, and then, when they least expected it, he brought as ugly a death as he could; to instill fear into those that remained and make them so afraid they would make mistakes. Errors of judgment that would ensure their death by his hand.

Michael's other problem was that he and God were also at war with one another since his precious, kind, and generous wife was diagnosed with cancer. Michael couldn't understand why this wonderful partner of thirty-two years was taken from him, and he felt that God was in some way punishing him for what he had done in Southeast Asia. These feelings were beginning to change as he realized that the holy war he found himself in was something God needed him for, and it was something his wife would not have been able to deal with. His anger was subsiding, and it was replaced with a kind of dialogue two friends might have. He was fighting a war, and the bits of information he received along the way told him he needed to move deeper and deeper into the maze of terrorists who had signed on to the jihad declared by Osama bin Laden.

He wiped his face with a clean white towel and dressed in his Levi jeans and a loose-fitting shirt to obscure any view of his concealed weapon. He would be leaving the country soon, so he needed a place to store his weapons in a safe place until his return, but before he could decide what to do, he wanted to talk with Tess. He was preparing for whatever might come and thinking a lot about her body and a very strong desire to touch her again. His cell phone rang, but it wasn't her…

Chapter One: Collateral Damage

Michael could sense by the voice of Chopper that he was in trouble, even though he attempted to speak like nothing was wrong.

"Hey Chopper, what's up?"

"I need to see you, John."

"No problem, where and when?" Michael questioned cheerfully.

"I'll meet you at the hangar at Francisco Bangoy. Can you make it today?" the nervous pilot questioned.

Michael faintly heard a thud like a handgun hitting his head. Then Chopper spoke again.

"Are you still in the Philippines?"

"I am, but I'm running a few errands. Any chance we can meet tomorrow, around two?" Michael lied into the phone, now sure that other ears were listening.

"That will be just fine; by the way, you left a few things at your hotel," Chopper said, hoping that his message was getting through. This was followed by another thudding sound.

Michael understood the gist of what Chopper was telling him, and it meant that he had some running around to do to help his new friend. Michael, knowing he had other ears listening, optimistically said, "See you then, Chop."

The soldier had to get moving to make the date. So, he quickly packed his belongings and a suitcase lined with money from his attack in Mindanao; then he headed to the Singapore airport.

The Machine was reactivating for an unforeseen engagement, and his plan of attack was already being formulated in his mind. Somehow, the enemy found his pilot and saw him as a way of getting to the leader of what they believed were the unknown forces who attacked them so successfully. Michael had to assume that his pilot, and new friend, was being tortured for information he didn't even have, but that made no difference to a group of thugs intent on hurting anyone, even women and children, for their cause. To them, collateral damage meant nothing.

It was late afternoon when he arrived back at the Pulchra Resort in Cebu City in a rental car. He went right to the counter and rang the bell. The manager, Ronald Albo appeared with a huge smile.

"Mister Doe, it is so good to see you again," the manager said happily.

"Good to be back in town. How's business?" Michael said to be social.

"Very Good, sir," Ronald responded.

"Someone left something for me," Michael said firmly.

"Yes, a large box in the back by our loading dock. Drive your car around the back of the hotel, and I will have a porter help you. The police have been here asking about you, but I gave them no details, Mr. Doe."

"Thanks, Ronald," Michael said with a small smile. He placed a hundred in Ronald's hand.

"Thank you, Mr. Doe. Thank you." The manager said enthusiastically.

He maneuvered his way to the back of the hotel, where a porter was already opening the loading dock door. Michael and the porter proceeded to load the heavy box into the back of his vehicle, slipped the porter a twenty, and then drove away. He looked down at his watch. It was five o'clock and his time was limited.

He found Pier four, North Reclamation Area in Cebu. His car was immediately surrounded by young boys with carts, wanting to be able to get paid for their assistance. Each boy called out to the stranger as he exited his car. Their efforts usually meant a cut of the fare for a fast boat transport. Michael pointed to a young boy who spoke perfect English.

"I'll need your cart to transport my goods to the fastest boat," Michael said to the boy.

"Okay, Joe, no problem. I'm Robert." I'll get your box, you pay at the boat. Okay, Joe?" The boy spoke quickly.

"You'll need my help with that," Michael said as he grabbed one end of the box. Robert picked up the other end, but never gave a clue to his customer that he was struggling. Michael followed behind as the boy wheeled the cargo to one of the Island Hopper transports. Inside the thirty-six-foot seacraft was an older Asian man in appearance, wearing old khaki pants with fish scales and blood smeared across the front right leg and a faded Hawaiian shirt that looked at least one size too big. He was moving around the older boat, making sure everything was in place before taking on passengers and setting out.

"Hey there! How long will it take to get me to Francisco Bangoy Airport?" Michael asked the boat Captain as he and the cart arrived at the dock.

"Maybe two hours' tops," the leather-faced Filipino responded.

"Okay, let's go," Michael told him.

"We wait for more passengers," the Captain said.

Michael pulled out two hundred-dollar bills and said, "Now."

"No problem, boss, we go right now," the Captain smiled.

Michael and the boy transferred the box to the boat. The old Filipino reached into his pocket, pulled out a ten-dollar bill, and gave it to the boy. Robert looked at it and screamed for joy; then he took off down the street, dancing with his cart. Michael turned to the old seaman with an inquisitive look.

"I just gave him about a month's wages. You overpaid me," the Captain said, smiling.

"You're a good man, Captain." Michael smiled back at him.

As they traveled, Michael couldn't help but marvel at the beauty that surrounded them. The lush landscape was breathtaking with island after island dotting a deep blue ocean tapestry. He looked down into the water, and it was so clear he could almost see the bottom of the ocean floor. He thought about his wife, Elle, and how much she liked the ocean. He wished he could have spent more time with her at the beach. He felt a tear escaping from his left eye and quickly wiped it with the back of his hand. His host saw him emote but kept quiet.

An hour passed before the Captain finally turned to Michael. "What's so important that you had to leave so quickly?"

"I have a friend in trouble, and I believe he's running out of time," Michael answered soberly.

"That serious?"

"I'm afraid so," Michael answered.

"What will you do?" the Captain asked.

Michael looked him straight in the eyes, "I'm going to kill a lot of really bad men tonight, and I'm going to make sure the rest of the bad men know it was me."

"Are you one of the guys that cleaned up the Mindanao jungles?"

"That would be me," Michael answered, watching the Captain's face, thinking he might have to start killing sooner than later.

"Well, there are a lot of us who want to say a big thank you. You're gonna need some help where you're going?" the old fisherman asked.

"Maybe just getting my crate to a taxi." He answered.

"I can do better than that. I have a car near the pier. Let me take you to wherever you need to go." The Captain offered sincerely.

"That would help. What's your name?" Michael asked.

"Amanaki, it's Polynesian. It means hope," the Captain said proudly. Then he asked, "What's yours?"

"Call me John." Michael lied with a straight face. Then Michael looked out over the beautiful blue ocean and marveled at God's handiwork. He remained quiet during the rest of the trip. His photographic memory recalled every detail of the hangar where he left Chopper, the details that would determine the success or failure of the upcoming operation.

The airport was a large square property with the international terminal occupying the front, where the major road made its connection. Behind the terminal were the runways, of which there were four. Behind that was a hangar and maintenance buildings, all located on the left side, with a large grassy area on the right. Then, in the very back of the airport property on the right side was a small terminal building for helicopters and a small hangar adjacent to it. He recalled a building on higher ground just to the right of the small heliport, which was not part of the airport property. This was where he could see the entire compound and where he needed to be to have a tactical advantage over an unknown number of enemy forces.

He looked up and spoke to God. “This isn’t gonna be easy, Lord, so any help you can give me will be appreciated.”

“John, I spent five years in the Filipino army, and I’m a pretty good shot,” Amanaki said, overhearing his passenger's prayer.

“This isn’t your war, my friend,” Michael replied with a small grin.

“I am begging to differ, John. We Filipinos are a Christian people, and the same threat that attacked America has been causing trouble here for many years. The Moro Islamic Liberation Front has been increasing its attacks on our people across the islands since 2000. Grenades were released into crowds, kidnappings, and murders. They are bad. Let me help you, John. I may not be younger than you, but I’m plenty fast sometimes.” Michael smiled at the old man's comment, then nodded and thought to himself, Okay, Lord, I get it. This is my hope, Amanaki.

Darkness overtook the speed boat just as it approached the no-wake area on its way to the pier. The two men worked together to tie off the boat and lift the box onto the dock. There were still young boys around, all eager to help for a few pesos. One boy, whom the Captain knew, ran over with a cart. The Captain handed him 2 pesos, and the two men placed the box on the boy's cart. The Captain told the boy to put the cart near his car. The two men loaded the crate into the back of Amanaki's old, rusted-out 1970 Volkswagen Hatchback. The car was orange in color, but so dirty it looked almost brown. The old man shut the back of the hatchback, and the men got inside.

They quickly made their way toward the airport. As they approached the entrance, Michael told his driver to go around to the side road just right of the terminal to a location that would be closer to the heliport hangar. They moved down the road until they arrived near an old building that had several dry-docked boats decorating the front with a weathered sign that Michael couldn't read. Amanaki translated the sign for his passenger.

"Banal na tubig bangka pagkumpuni, it is called Holy Water Boat Repair. I know the owner; his name is Joseph, a good man."

"Great name. Think he'll mind the intrusion?" Michael asked.

"I'll give him a call," Amanaki answered.

The Captain pulled out his cell phone and spoke in Tegalog. When he got off the phone, he said, "Joseph is coming with his oldest son, Adam. They want to help."

"Amanaki!" Michael declared.

"What can I tell you, they're coming," he responded to Michael's look.

Michael went over to the box, opened it, and pulled out binoculars. He went behind the boat repair building, which gave him an unobstructed view of the hangar down below. He hid behind one of the many boats being stored in the rear area behind the building, pulled up the binoculars, and did a preliminary inspection of the hangar. It looked deserted, but Michael was not leaving anything to chance. He would be doing his own brand of reconnaissance. So, he went back to the box, pulled out his camouflage gear, and changed quickly into all black. He applied the lampblack powder to his face and hands. Next, he secured his 380 handgun with a silencer in place and slid it into a side holster, added a twelve-inch hunting knife with a sheath to his utility belt, and placed Betty, his self-made killing device, onto his finger.

Joseph and his son Adam pulled up in an old white Chevrolet utility van. Michael looked them over, evaluating their ability to soldier if necessary. Amanaki introduced them to their new leader.

“What do you need us to do, John?” Joseph asked.

“For now, just keep your eyes open. I don’t think their forces have arrived yet, but I’ll feel better once I get a lay of the land. If I'm not back in twenty minutes, you all get the hell out of here.” Michael instructed them.

The part of Michael known as The Machine took over as he made his way down the back side of the boat repair to the rear of the heliport hangar. There he stood quietly as he waited for an unfamiliar sound to present itself. He had learned years before to be patient, then it came, the sound of someone lighting a cigarette and inhaling that first bit of smoke. He moved toward the sound and saw white smoke just around the corner of the hangar. This foot soldier wasn’t expecting an attack; he was just waiting impatiently for the rest of the group to arrive. The Machine brought Betty to attention, and once she was locked into place, he took his left hand and covered the man's mouth, and at the same time inserted the blade deep into the right side of his neck. Betty found her mark in the right carotid artery. Then he gently lowered the limp body slowly to the ground without making a noise to cause alarm. He moved onward around the building and, finding no one else on the exterior, he moved to where the hangar door could be seen. There were voices of men speaking in another language. It was a conversation between only two people. By the sound, Michael perceived they were about three feet into the room. They turned in surprise as Michael stood right in the doorway, his weapon out and ready to deliver a silent message. The first shot entered the right eye of the man facing him; the second blew the kneecap off the other soldier's left leg and dropped him screaming in pain. If there were more soldiers, this guy's screams would have them there in seconds, ready for battle. Michael stood ready for all-out war. This surprise attack would not be anticipated, and it was just what the Machine was counting on. However, there was no response to the screaming. That was good. He wanted intelligence from the survivor, anything that might give him a bit of an advantage.

"How many are here?" he asked with the tip of his favorite weapon, Betty, piercing the skin under the chin of the man moaning in pain.

"Three," the man answered weakly.

Michael sat on the floor near the dead man and the wounded one. He was watching the face of the survivor as he pulled the dead man's hand between them. He pulled out the foot-long hunting knife and placed it at the distal phalanges of the index finger. Then he took his left hand and pounded the back of the blade, which caused the finger tip to disengage.

The Machine spoke softly to his enemy. “Anyone who touches my friends must pay a very high price.”

He went back to the hand and continued removing the last joint of each finger. The sound of crushing bone brought chills to the wounded soldier whose eyes widened with each finger-tip removed.

He fearfully thought to himself, I have never been instructed how to respond to this kind of brutality.

When all the tips were removed, Michael turned all his attention to his prisoner. “What’s your name, soldier?” Michael asked calmly as he gathered up the removed fingers into a pile.

“Navid,” he answered, now stricken with fear.

“What does it mean, Navid?” Michael questioned.

“It means good news,” Navid answered.

“Perhaps you can provide me with good news, Navid. I want to know who your leader is and when he will be coming to the hangar with my friend. I know you could resist me, at which point I will be forced to remove all your fingers, or you could spare yourself such horrible pain and just give me what I want.” Michael remarked with a smile.

“They will arrive in the early morning,” Navid responded, still grimacing in pain from his bleeding knee.

“From where?” Michael continued his questioning.

“Microtel Inn, about six kilometers south of the airport,” the wounded soldier replied and then asked, “Are you one of the group who attacked Mindanao?”

Michael nodded with a smile and remarked, "There were only two of us."

The wounded sentry's eyes got very big and looked even more frightened.

"How many in your group and who is the leader?" Michael asked.

"There are six of us who came from Iran at the request of our leaders to investigate the attack on Mindanao. We have a group of twenty Muslim Filipinos. They found out about the helicopter pilot who helped you in Mindanao and brought him to our leader, Mansoor Amoli." Navid answered and then queried. "May I ask you a question?"

"Of course," Michael answered politely.

"Are you the one they spoke of, the one that kills and mutilates our people, the one they call the monster?" Navid asked.

"I am the monster, Navid, but you have been very cooperative, so I will kill you before I take your fingers."

Navid's face, beaded with stress, showed clearly his fear of dying.

Michael continued, "I must send a clear message that anyone who touches my friends will never touch anything again. Do you understand?"

Navid nodded his understanding. Michael allowed him to finish nodding, then put a silent but deadly bullet into his head. He checked his body, found a cell phone, and placed it in his pocket. He methodically cut off all of Navid's fingers and went outside and did the same to the soldier by the hangar. He carried the finger tips in a canvas bag he found in the hangar and made his way back to the boat repair shop.

Michael sat with his force of three to decide what might be the best way to confront the twenty-one remaining enemy forces. The men couldn't help but notice the blood beginning to soak the canvas. They stared at the bag and then at Michael. The Machine said firmly, "I'm sending them a message." Michael could see the fear in their eyes, but went on to explain to his novice soldiers that waiting for the enemy to arrive might mean the death of his friend. The best plan was to blitz them at three in the morning when all of them should be asleep. They would not expect such an audacious move.

Joseph thought for a moment, then announced to Michael, "The night manager of the Microtel Inn and I are old fishing buddies. He should be working tonight."

"That's great! All I'll need is a manager's key card and the room numbers. Do you think your friend can do that?" Michael asked.

"I think so," Joseph replied.

"What about us, John?" Amanaki asked.

"Adam, you wait in the van but keep the engine running." Michael wanted the kid as far from the attack as possible.

"Amanaki and Joseph each take a revolver, wait at the end of the hallway, if anyone comes out other than me, shoot him." Both men nodded.

Michael went through the box and picked out a weapon for each man, both with silencers. He gave them each an extra clip. He thought to himself, Lord, please let them be good shots.

Michael took out four ten-round clips for his 380 and a smoke grenade if he needed to simulate a fire or to create cover for his attack. He hooked everything to his utility belt and said, "Let's move out."

All the men got into the van and headed down the road toward the hotel with Adam behind the wheel. They were silent for most of the short trip, with Michael studying the faces of his unconventional army.

Amanaki broke the silence. "We should say a prayer before we do this."

The men agreed, so Amanaki began. "Lord, watch over us this night and help us to get John's friend from these very bad men. We ask this through Christ our Lord, Amen."

The six kilometers went by quickly, with each man understanding what was expected of them.

Chapter Two: Extraction

Chopper was becoming aware of his surroundings when he was struck in the head again. It was a powerful punch to the jaw that made the whole side of his face ache, and suddenly the motel room began to spin out of control until he was lost in unconsciousness. His assailant was Jazeer, the right-hand man for Mansoor Amoli. He looked over at his leader, who gave him a signal to stop.

Mohammed Jazeer was a soldier of Osama Bin Laden and had a reputation for relishing in the pain of his enemy before killing them. He had decapitated many hostages, all in the name of Allah, and after 9/11, made his way to the Philippines to activate an Al-Qaeda cell. He was away in Hong Kong with his leader, Mansoor Amoli, when their cell in Mindanao was attacked. When Jazeer discovered what had happened, his desire for revenge was uncontrollable. However, his superior, Amoli, was in charge and tempered Jazeer's rage.

Mansoor Amoli was a very intelligent man who didn't like getting his hands dirty. He was a good delegator for the jihadist movement, and his men were zealots for the cause. They were known throughout the organization to do anything he asked of them without question. When the pilot regained consciousness, Amoli asked for more information. Chopper refused to give any details about the number of infidels but kept repeating that his life was not of any value to the group he transported.

"I'm just a pilot to them, nothing more. They probably won't even come tomorrow." Chopper tried to explain.

This comment caused Jazeer's fist to knock him out again.

"We will see pilot man, either way, tomorrow you will die with the infidels or without them." Mansoor declared to the unconscious man.

It was close to midnight when Jazeer and Mansoor retired to the adjoining room for the night. Their captive, tied to a chair, was beaten severely but made no sound for fear of continued abuse. The clock in the room said 12:59 AM. Chopper regained consciousness, and his torturers had gone off to sleep. He struggled against the ropes that held him for almost an hour without interruption. Unable to get loose and exhausted, he finally dropped off to sleep.

The white van was parked on the side of the building, not visible from the motel lobby. Michael handed Joseph the dead man's cell phone, and Joseph called his friend inside the motel. In Tegalic, he described the capture of the pilot and told him what they needed. The manager whispered into the phone that there were a few men still hanging around in the lobby.

"I'll pass you what you need. Just come up to the counter by yourself, and I'll book you a room. Your key card will be able to open every door on the list," the manager explained.

Adam remained in the van as ordered. The three men exited the vehicle. Michael, all in black, told Joseph to get the key and the room numbers and then make his way to the side entrance to open the door and let them in.

Joseph was visibly nervous and made the sign of the cross. Michael grabbed Joseph by his arm and said, "You're going in to get a room, nothing more. If these animals even get a hint that something is up, all bets are off, understand?"

Joseph nodded, then said calmly, “You both wait by the door.” He turned and made his way inside. Michael and Amanaki made their way to the side entrance, but it was taking longer than Michael had calculated.

The Machine went into alert mode. When the door clicked open, Michael caught a glimpse of someone moving behind Joseph. A second later, the body dropped as The Machine's weapon discharged two silent killing projectiles into the man's head. The sound of the body hitting the floor would be enough to bring anyone else in the vicinity running. So, Michael carefully moved his soldiers to one side of the narrow entrance and made his way toward the lobby to meet the enemy. One enemy combatant was already making a move toward the sound, his hand reaching for a weapon, while the other, half asleep, only looked over his shoulder. The night manager, seeing Michael, ducked under the counter for safety. Michael's weapon spat out two more deadly rounds at the first man, dropping him immediately, and caught the other man, who still had not made any sense out of what was happening, with a bullet to the side of his head. Michael then moved into the lobby to ensure the coast was clear.

He made his way to the counter, looked over, and said to the shaking manager, “Get rid of the bodies.”

The army of three entered the elevator and pressed the button up to the top floor. Michael wanted to find his friend first and, using the list provided by the manager, estimated where he might be located. He thought it was interesting that these Muslim radicals always seemed to put themselves on the higher floors and their soldiers on the floors below. He smiled to himself, Death is coming, and I don't care the order.

His new recruits had their guns at the ready as Michael slipped the key card into the door. A green light appeared, followed by a clicking sound. He moved the door handle down and slipped quietly into the very dark room. Michael could smell blood as he passed the bathroom and found himself in the sitting area of the suite. His night vision improving by the second brought an image of his friend tied securely to a chair, his head down. Michael slipped his hand around Chopper's head and held his mouth to ensure not a sound was made. Chopper's eyes opened, frightened, but relaxed quickly when he heard the Machine's voice tell him to stay calm. The hunting knife sliced through the rope behind him, first at the wrist and then at his feet.

Michael signaled to Chopper, doing a body count with his fingers, and Chopper responded with two fingers. Michael moved to the bedroom on the left, entered and exited a moment later, the only one sound barely audible. He moved to the next room, prepared to duplicate his actions.

Mansoor Amoli was sleeping well. He was dreaming of getting back home to Iran, to a wife he truly loved who was totally devoted to him and to his two handsome twin sons. He awoke in horror, a wash rag shoved in his mouth, just as a silent bullet entered his right knee. Then, before he even had a chance to respond, the other knee exploded from the muffled bullet of the silenced 380 handgun. Chopper was standing behind Michael and trying to get past him to attack the man who ordered his torture. Michael held him back, saying, "Get the rope and tie him up really well. I'll be back for both of you in a little while."

The Machine descended and entered one room, then the next, quietly reducing the odds. There were four more rooms on the third floor that required his attention. He key-carded one room to find a soldier standing in the middle of the room staring at him as he entered. His handgun sputtered out two rounds between his eyes. The body dropping to the floor made just enough noise to arouse the other three men in the room. The seasoned soldier had to move quickly to eliminate the threat and reduce the possibility of waking the whole motel. He dropped the second combatant as he lunged to retrieve his weapon. The other two were trying to get out of bed as Michael decisively put them to sleep forever. Room by room, The Machine reduced the odds.

The second floor had the remaining rooms. He encountered three soldiers watching a porn channel as he quietly entered the room. They were totally unaware of the stranger's presence until blood spray hit their faces. It was all over a second later. He stepped out of the room to see Joseph pointing his weapon, his hand shaking the whole time. Michael signaled that there was only one room to go by, making a one-finger gesture. He went to the last room, found them all asleep when he discovered them, and dead when he left. He told Joseph and Amanaki to go back to the van and wait for him.

Michael went back into the room, removed a pillowcase, and proceeded to remove the fingertips of the dead men. He retraced his movement from room to room, ensuring he had all the fingers of all the men placed into the blood-soaked cloth bag. His task ended back in the room of Mansoor, who appeared to be unconscious and badly beaten by his former prisoner.

"Glad you didn't kill him, because I have other plans for him," Michael said to Chopper, whose hands were bloody.

"Let me kill the bastard," Chopper responded.

"This will be one of those rare circumstances where he will be more valuable to send a message alive rather than dead. I'll need him to provide me with some information, but first I need to finish gathering fingers." Michael's last word came out as all his attention was focused on Mansoor, who woke up just in time to catch Michael's last words.

Amoli was sure he could withstand any torture he had learned in his study of interrogation by the American government, so, as he prepared himself for what he thought would happen. Michael stood over his enemy while wiping off the blood from his hunting knife. He did not even acknowledge the tied terrorist but proceeded to cut the terrorist's pinky finger at the base. The terrorist tried to scream through the washcloth in his mouth, but Michael took the finger-filled pillowcase and opened it so the terrorist could catch a glimpse of what was in the bag. Then Michael dropped Mansoor's still-moving finger in with the rest he had acquired. The terror in his eyes made Michael sure he would be able to get as much information as this soldier had.

"Who sent you?" he asked; his knife poised to strike at the next digit. He pulled the wash rag from his mouth.

"His name is Aqeel Gabany; that is the name I know," Mansoor said weakly. He was not willing to sacrifice another digit for the jihad movement; all his answers came quickly.

"Where is he?"

"He is in the United States," he answered.

"What is his plan?"

"He said we should first eliminate you and your team of killers, and then proceed to Washington, D.C. It is there we are to meet him for further instructions. Something to do with politics, but he did not specify to me. He said I would get more information when I return." Mansoor answered without hesitation.

"Do you have a family, Mansoor?" Michael gently asked, staring at him.

"I do," he said meekly.

"Would you like to see them again?" Michael questioned his voice, almost soothing.

"I would," he responded.

"Children?"

"Two sons, twins."

"How old are they?" He queried further, getting more intimate.

"Four years old," came the answer.

"I'll tell you what I'm going to do for you. I'm going to send you home to your family, but understand what happens to anyone who touches those I love or call friends. They will all die just as all these men died." He opened the pillowcase and showed him again the bag of fingers.

"If I find you have helped your radical jihadist group in any way with information about my friends or me. I will find your family, and I will dissect them in front of you while they scream in agony until they are a quivering mass at your feet, and then I will leave you unable to walk so that you must watch them die in front of you. Do you believe I am capable of this, Mansoor?" He asked softly.

The soldier wept openly at the visual he might have to endure with the full knowledge that this madman would be sure to carry it out.

"DO YOU?" Michael screamed into his face, making sure his message was clearly heard.

"Yes, yes, yes," he whimpered.

"So now you will work for me...right?" His question was more like a demand.

The response came back, "Yes."

Michael proceeded to detail what he expected from his new employee. "First contact Aqeel and request transport to the United States, as you have an important message which needs your leader's immediate attention. You will transport the fingers of your comrades to this Aqeel, so he understands the monster he is at war with and that there is nothing I won't do to hurt him and his jihadists. You will refer to me in the plural. They...Them. I will be calling you from time to time for information. You will always keep me appraised of where you are and what you are doing. Make sure what you tell me is accurate in every way because if any part of it is wrong, there is no place in the world you and your family will be able to hide to avoid the consequences I described to you. Do we have an understanding?"

Mansoor nodded.

"For your loyalty to me, I will let you live and protect you and your family."

Somewhere during his brief interrogation, Mansoor decided that his life and that of his family was more important than the jihad he was so loyal to for so many years. He thought to himself, Yes, I will do whatever you ask of me.

The Machine looked over at Chopper and whispered, "They won't be touching you ever again."

Michael tied off Mansoor's legs to stop the bleeding. He told Chopper to wait outside the room. He sat on the floor next to the terrorist. "The God I serve is a God of love and one of forgiveness. It is important for you to know what the truth is and what isn't. I'm not going to make you read the Bible, but it would serve you well to know what is of God and what isn't. I will help you in this search for answers, but deceive me, and you will find that I am not as forgiving as God, and your family will die horrible deaths."

He called Chopper back in and instructed him to take Mansoor to his soldiers waiting in the white van on the side entrance of the motel. When I'm done here, we'll take him to the hospital. After the two departed, Michael went through the room for weapons and cash. He wasn't disappointed; the top drawer of the hotel dresser had a briefcase, and inside it was over $100,000 in U.S. dollars. He surmised it must be a payoff for the soldiers, once they eliminated him. Next to the case was a black Beretta 9mm with a five-inch barrel. Michael released the magazine to inspect it. It held fifteen rounds. The weapon was semi-automatic and weighed about two pounds. At the end of the barrel was a quick-release silencer. Michael liked the feel of the weapon, and he was very aware of its killing potential. Yes, he thought to himself, this would be good to have. He slipped the weapon into the briefcase and exited the room.

Before leaving the hotel, he approached the manager, "In an hour, contact the police and tell them you were told to wait before calling or you would be killed."

He started to exit the front entrance, where the van was now waiting, when Michael noticed the camera over the door. He went back behind the counter and pulled the tapes out of the camera recorder, then took his 380 and shot multiple holes into the adjacent computer. He pulled out twenty $100 bills and gave them to the manager. "This should cover the damages."

Chapter Three: Transmission

The FBI and CIA had initially issued an alert for information regarding the whereabouts of Michael Angelino when deaths began to occur in Galveston and Mexico City. However, with intelligence of new terrorist attacks overseas, as well as reports that Michael Angelino was dead, his overall importance seemed to fall off the radar rather quickly.

The most notable squelched homeland attack was in December 2001. English citizen Richard Reid tried to blow up a plane with a shoe bomb, which would forever change security in airports around the world and had government agencies scrambling to come up with a way to prevent another 9/11. This would also make traveling for everyday citizens a much longer process just to get to the terminal on time. As for Michael, he needed to make sure his fake identifications could muster scrutiny. He spent almost two weeks working with his source in Texas and having new identification documents made for David Devlin, a traveling salesman. Once his passport and other identification cards arrived, he would be ready to board a flight back to the United States. While he waited, he heard a news report that another terrorist attempt was found out in time to prevent a disaster. He was glad to hear that. He thought about the jihadist groups and the success they had with 9/11, and he thought this attack on planes was sure to continue.

Assistant to the head of the terrorist task force and new girlfriend to Michael Angelino, Tess, received notification from the Philippines that a motel near the airport was the scene of a horrific mass murder. Upon hearing the gruesome details, she surmised that her new boyfriend was at work. She tried reaching him but was unable to get a response from her many messages. This always made her worry. The silence meant he was under fire, missing, or dead; none of which gave her any consolation.

Ted entered her office and asked, "Has he contacted you yet?"

She shook her head, annoyed by the comment, and said, "There is no way Michael Angelino could be involved in any of this."

"Well, he seems to be at it again." He said as he threw down the faxed information from their Philippines office.

"I've seen it, Ted, and the report says that it was a group of men in black, not an older gentleman by himself." She attempted to make his accusations appear silly and incomprehensible.

Ted was going out of his way to demonize her ex-boss. He knew they were close. Chet Avery told him as much. Ted found her to be very attractive and almost came out and said it on occasion, but Tess pretended not to pick up on it. The man she loved was out there somewhere, and all she could think of…was whether he was alright?

The mastermind of the recent terror attacks foiled by the Machine was Aqeel Gabany. He was an American-educated Iranian with a hatred for everything that represented the Western way of living, particularly regarding their women. However, it didn't start out that way. He was attending the New York College, NYU, where he met and fell in love with Breanne Tevoli, a very modern-minded woman from Pennsylvania with aspirations of being on the Broadway stage. He met her in a speech class and was immediately smitten.

She thought he would be a nice distraction from her rigorous schedule because he was very handsome with an Omar Sharif look about him. They began dating during freshman year, and by the time they were seniors, he had expressed his sincere love for her.

Breanne laughed in his face. “I can't get serious with you, Aqeel. I'll be going to auditions and working on my career. It's a world where you don't belong.”

This hurt the young student who spoke to a few of his friends about being rejected. They suggested he attend their Iranian club on campus. Once there, he was surprised to find more than a few members who confessed to being used by these American women and who mentioned that it would never happen if Sharia Law was in place. This law stated that a woman could be stoned to death for having intercourse out of wedlock or for dishonoring her man. Aqeel thought he could convince her that they could have a life together, so he contacted Breanne and asked her out for dinner. She felt he was being too persistent and that she would need to be blunt with him, so she agreed to a final date.

With school just ending and Aqeel planning a trip home to Iran, he felt it might be his last chance to convince Breanne of his love. They met at their favorite place, the Babbo Ristorante near Washington Square Park. Aqeel used to meet her there after rehearsals at the Judson Poets Theater, which was just down the street from the NYU Islamic center where he had become quite active.

The dinner wasn't going too well, and Breanne could sense that Aqeel was losing his temper after she indicated her plans were to move to Los Angeles after graduation. She suggested they walk through the park to avoid a confrontation in the restaurant. As they walked, Aqeel could feel his anger reaching a boiling point. He looked down and noticed his shoe was untied. So, he knelt to tie his lace. His eye caught sight of a stone, so he picked it up. His head was swirling with anger. Breanne kept walking ahead of him. Without thinking, he took the stone and struck her in the back of the head. She became disoriented from the blow, and before she could recover, he struck her again, which brought her to the ground. Aqeel was out of his mind as he repeated the attack, striking her again and again until she was dead. In a panic at what he had done, he took the bloodied rock and went back to his apartment, cleaned himself up, and went to the airport to catch the plane for Iran. By the time the bludgeoned body was discovered, and the police arrived at the crime scene, Aqeel was deplaning in Tehran.

The education he received at NYU and his ever-growing knowledge of the United States, its culture, along with his undocumented degree from Al Qaeda over the next few years, helped him to gain power and move him into a diplomatic position. A position where he could control others who would carry out acts of terror at his command. This was where he felt he was destined to be. He became a consultant to Jihadi forces, including Osama Bin Laden, a kind of inside man.

The group of American mercenaries who prevented the second major attack against America in Galveston must be dead by now at the hands of my forces, he thought to himself. He was sure that using the helicopter pilot as bait would draw out the American soldiers. Aqeel was laughing to himself at what he had accomplished and how easily he could predict the actions of his enemy. Their rules of war would be their undoing.

He was not surprised when the intercom from his secretary indicated that Mansoor Amoli had arrived. The diplomat was expecting his soldier.

"Send him in," Aqeel spoke into the intercom.

The look on his face changed as Mansoor wobbled in on crutches, his hand wrapped with bandages. He was carrying a large blood-soaked pillowcase.

"Mansoor, what has happened to you?" He asked, very surprised.

The wounded man said, "I was told to deliver a message to you."

"What message?" he questioned, still puzzled.

Mansoor poured the contents of the blood-soaked bag onto the floor and watched as his superior recoiled in horror. The disengaged fingers formed a pile almost six inches high. Mansoor watched Aqeel's face as he spoke, "Our enemy said that this will be how they respond to any further threats against anyone who has helped them."

"Who are these madmen?" Aqeel screeched his voice going up an octave.

"They are called The Machine, some call them Monster, and they said they're coming for you."

Mansoor watched Aqeel's face twitch as his ears heard the last sentence. "They told me to tell you that they are going to kill you very slowly so that you will have time to feel the kind of pain the innocent American families felt on 9/11."

Aqeel screamed expletives into the room, his fists raised in anger. After the outburst, he looked over at Mansoor, who was struggling to remain standing. "Mansoor, these American men let you live. Explain."

Mansoor proceeded to describe his torture, exaggerating all of it to get sympathy from his superior. "Their leader said I am their first and only survivor and that if they find me again, they will remove the rest of my fingers and then my head, but I do not fear these infidels, and as soon as I am able, I request to be sent back to kill all of them. They took my finger, the bastards."

"Yes, Mansoor, we shall see, but for now, you must get better, my brother." Aqeel consoled his soldier.

The fighter told his superior that he could still be of value in their jihad by providing him with information about their forces' size and descriptions of those he saw while their captive.

"Yes, this will be invaluable. First, you must be seen by our doctors, then provide my staff with as much information as you can recall. I will arrange a flight for you to visit your family and recuperate. Mansoor, these forces can't be everywhere. They will not be able to stop our next major attack. Soon Britain will bow to Allah. We will kill thousands right under the city of London." Aqeel blustered to his subordinate.

Mansoor bowed in gratitude and began to leave the room. He suddenly turned back toward Aqeel and added, "They also said that their God will be sure that they accomplish this goal."

After his wounded warrior left the room, Aqeel stared at the pile of fingertips as consternation began to overwhelm him. He started to sweat as he pondered what he could do to get control over this situation. He finally sat at his desk, went through his contact list, and phoned Chet Avery.

"Hello, Avery, here," came the voice through the phone.

"Who are these bastards and how many soldiers do they have at their disposal?" Aqeel demanded to know.

"What are you doing calling me here? I'll call you from my burner phone in five minutes." Chet whispered emphatically into the receiver. He stepped out and made his way into the courtyard, the center of the Pentagon structure.

He pressed the speed dial for Aqeel and waited only a second to hear "Who's doing this?"

"I wish I knew. At first, I thought it was one of my old agents, but he's been at a desk for over 30 years and frankly is not capable of such devastation. Anyway, he took a job with the Secret Service and got caught in the crossfire down in Galveston; his charred body was pulled out of a vehicle." Chet lied, trying to convince himself of that possibility, as he spoke. "I believe that the CIA has set up a counter terrorist task force with Navy Seals and Marine Force Reconnaissance soldiers, and I believe whoever has let them loose has given them a green light to do whatever is necessary to end your operation," Chet concluded with a hint of gladness in his voice.

Aqeel picked up on it immediately and screamed into the phone, "If anything happens to me, it will also be your undoing, and I will release the photos of your perversion, so don't forget it." He hung up the phone, still staring at the digit remains of his entire Jihadi force.

Michael had just finished packing for his trip to Dulles when he received a call from his new contact, Mansoor. The call was brief.

"Something is going down in England, and it could affect all of Europe. I believe it may have something to do with the Tube." The new informant wasted no time making himself useful to his leader.

Mansoor felt sure that something was brewing. It came right from Aqeel in a passing statement.

"One more thing, I am reading about your Jesus, and I am puzzled. Perhaps we can discuss it later?" He asked.

"Be open to what you read and check historical documents as well, because Jesus was a real man," Michael told his informant.

"I will, boss," Mansoor said and hung up.

This meant Michael would not be going home after all. He changed his itinerary with the counter agent at the airport. The next flight was leaving in three hours for Heathrow. He couldn't afford any distractions, and that meant not contacting Tess. He shut off his phone and began to devise a plan to infiltrate the enemy. Going deep undercover would be a high-risk operation if he could pull it off at all. It also meant no transmissions. He needed to be off the grid completely. He would need to build a cover and change his appearance, and that would take a bit of time. So, upon arrival in England, Michael Angelino disappeared into the population of over six million people and became just another face in the crowd.

He spent his first month alone, allowing his hair and beard to grow considerably and reading the Koran until he almost had it completely memorized. He found an apartment in the area of Soho, walking distance from the Mosque. He purchased clothes at least two sizes too big to give himself a smaller appearance.

Chapter Four: Clandestine

By the middle of March 2003, with reports of weapons of mass destruction unaccounted for within the country of Iraq and bipartisan support from Congress, President Bush and Prime Minister Tony Blair jointly launched an all-out assault on that country. The less than three-month war resulted in the death of Saddam Hussein's two sons and Hussein's removal as the leader of their country. Although the war itself was relatively brief, the results did not stop Al Qaeda from continuing its attempts at terrorism around the world.

It was May of 2003 when U.S. Officials arrested Lyman Faris and then charged him with conspiracy. News reports indicated it was a plot to collapse the Brooklyn Bridge. His plan was foiled by the joint efforts of Interpol, the FBI, and the CIA, and the coordinated efforts of Tess Lamia. Tess was working around the clock with both the FBI and the CIA to ensure that everyone's I's were dotted, and their T's were crossed, and most importantly, that each knew what the other was doing. Her role as a liaison was instrumental in the ongoing war on terror, and her level of professionalism was noticed by her superiors, especially Chet Avery and Ted Hobson.

Ted would have liked to take their relationship from professional to personal, but he could sense that she was still mourning the apparent loss of her old boss. Ted was disappointed in losing Michael as a potential mercenary against Al Qaeda, but after the Philippines attack at the Microtel Inn and no information on the old agent at all in almost six months, he wondered where Michael's body would be found.

Tess went from denial that Michael was dead, to anger that he hadn't called her at least one last time. She had prayed to God to please bring him back to her. She began bargaining and negotiating, willing to make a personal sacrifice if God would do this one thing for her. She reached the depression stage, and this is where she remained. Her appetite was gone, and every night she cried herself to sleep remembering his touch, his lips, and his face smiling up at her while making love. She just couldn't bring herself to accept what seemed obvious to everyone else within the bureau.

An elderly balding man with a full gray beard walking with a cane, who went by the name Ben Amir, made his way down the road from his apartment to a small mosque at 10 Berwick Street. This had become a ritual for him and a place where many Muslims gathered to discuss their ever-changing world since the attacks in New York. British intelligence recruited local Muslims to watch with scrupulous eyes for signs of terrorism within the local population. The mosque was also a place where radical Muslims, followers of Bin Laden, planned ways of keeping the Western world away from their homeland. It was this faction the old man was interested in, and he had established himself as one of their family, a harmless old man seeking a closeness to Allah whom the radicals could talk to freely without fear of exposure.

Michael worked very hard to gain acceptance within the mosque, and his outward appearance made him look quite docile. Yet his life was one of constant physical training with a minimum of three hours a day working out in his small studio apartment in the heart of Soho. The baggy clothes made him appear frail and smaller than he was, and the limp and the cane made him appear weak. He was, in fact, in the best shape of his life. He purposely planted himself in the small district known as Soho, which had an interesting and storied history.

During the late fifties, Soho became the initial area for the beatnik generation. A locale where theater artists, painters, and poets gathered at many of the coffee shops and bars to discuss philosophy, beauty, and love. Drinking and partaking in the many brothels made Soho a premier red-light district, which, over the years, kept it from being a bright attraction for tourists or a sought-after area for business and residents. This allowed immigrants to flood the zone upon their arrival in Britain. The mosque in the heart of this area is where Ben took residence. He was sure that the bohemian attitude of the local Soho population was what gave the radical Muslims their justification to kill these infidels. They were only waiting for the perfect time to exact jihad against the very people they had befriended after migrating.

Michael spent every day of the last five months in the mosque on Berwick Street and spent hours in prayer in the sight of all who entered. It was during his time there that Imam Raashid Mohammad had indicated to his congregation that there was a British intolerance for their faith that was a direct result of the 9/11 attacks. The Machine's sixth sense told him that the Imam could not be trusted and needed to be under surveillance.

Ben found a group of seven young men who spoke of violence against all infidels and decided to discuss the Koran with them. He spent countless hours memorizing their holy book, in the hope he could persuade these young men to find a peaceful solution to their uncontrollable anger. Michael's faith had saved him so many years before, and he prayed that somehow, he might be a positive influence on these misguided young radicals. This wasn't his usual approach, but reading and thinking about God each day gave him a different focus. He was trying to reach their souls. However, they told him that the days of waiting were over, and that Allah wanted them to invoke justice on the infidels, who were leading decadent, disgusting lives and who had no right to life.

One of the young men, Ali, told Michael, "Look around, old man, and see where we live. It is filled with drunkards and harlots;

these people will never convert to Islam, and for that reason, we are justified to execute them."

"Listen, Ali, Allah is the judgment on the world, and we must be an example of goodness and holiness to those who do not know Him in the hope that through us they will convert to our faith," Michael argued.

"Ben, you are an old man who believes that change will come one day. We believe change must come now," the young man asserted.

"What can you young men accomplish?" Michael asked, hoping for more details about the orders that must be coming from their Imam.

"The underground system here in London is a perfect place to kill many infidels and send a message to the West that their involvement in the Middle East must stop, or many more thousands will die." Ali went on to declare quietly. "Our group has been chosen to sacrifice ourselves for the wishes of Allah."

"Please, Ali, 9/11 has only brought more death and destruction to the Middle East. Why do you think Japan's emperor called America a sleeping giant during World War II? America's resolve to rid the world of the jihadists will also kill many of us who only want freedom to practice our faith. They will make no distinction between young or old, activist or peaceful. My boy, your life must be worth more than to sacrifice it to cause the death of a few thousand people. How much more powerful will you be by using your voice to protest the injustice our people are experiencing because of the likes of Bin Laden?" Ben liked the young man and hoped his words might persuade Ali to alter his course of action.

Michael tried to reason in his own mind how these young, intelligent men could be manipulated to a course of action that meant certain death by their suicide, with no regard to the innocent women and children who would be among their victims. Unfortunately, he knew the power of intense indoctrination. These men were probably being groomed from the time they were ten to twelve years of age. Taught that the West was the cause of all their problems and the reason their country suffered economically over the years. Despite his efforts, Michael was not making any headway in changing the young zealot's mind. He began to realize that he could not alter their distorted views. If this group wasn't going to change their course of action, then they would be killed by the very man who was trying to save them.

Michael, the soldier who truly understood war, knew when talks were no longer effective. He began his surveillance of the group when he first became aware of their intentions, but his desire to somehow change their minds let his usually keen eye lapse. He did not consider that there might be more than one group within the mosque that could be of potential danger to London. His notebook recorded each young man's daily routine from the moment they got up until they went to bed. His next course of action was to establish a place to eliminate the enemy quickly, without time for them to carry out their plan for destruction.

The London Subway, or the Underground as they called it, was the oldest subway system in the world. It began in late 1863 and to date has traveled over 408 kilometers with over three million passengers a day. If the enemy wanted to exact tremendous death and destruction, this would be the ideal place to do it. The subway system was broken up into six zones. Zone six was the farthest outside London, and each zone brought you closer to the center, which was zone one. This would be the biggest kill area filled with thousands of locals and tourists from all over the world, and Michael shuddered at the thought of the number of potential deaths. He decided he could not wait another day to move. He would take them out all at once, and he needed to do it as quickly as possible.

The seven young men showed up at the mosque together every morning for Salat, which is the call for prayer done five times a day. The Machine decided that he would not kill them in their house of worship. He had researched the neighborhood and found the perfect spot. He positioned himself on the roof at Number 6 Walker Court, a building just past 99 Berwick, very far down the street, but a location with an optimal view of the front of the Islamic Center. He had acquired a British sniper rifle the UKP 23,000 from an ex-member of British Intelligence for close to $10,000 American dollars. It was a bit over-priced, but it was terrorist money, so he really didn't mind. The rifle was designed for long-distance shooting and fired an 8.59mm bullet. It weighed 6.8kg, and in the hands of The Machine, it could hit a human-sized target from 1400 meters. Michael had positioned himself less than three football fields from his targets, and the rifle had a suppressor so that his location would never even be suspected.

The Machine was in his nest since four in the morning, the sun was behind him, which was optimal but still not visible, but his vision was improving as daybreak approached. He saw the young men beginning to gather near the entrance.

Michael looked up momentarily and let God know his reasoning, "I gave them every opportunity to stop, Lord. Now there is no other choice. Please forgive me for what I must do." With that said, he looked through the scope and prepared for action.

The seven young men arrived and stood outside the mosque close together, talking. Ali lit a cigarette and handed the lighter to one of the other men. In that instant, the young man's head exploded. Before any of them could react to protect themselves, a succession of rifle rounds riddled the remaining six until they all went down into a pile of wasted youth. The bullet that ended Ali's life caused the trained killer to tear after the task was completed. Using the high-powered scope, he viewed the dead. Mission complete, he thought to himself. The caring was something he would try to avoid in the future; he knew that it would cause hesitation, and that could mean his own death. He left the nest, hid his weapon inside the closet of his apartment behind two loose wood slats. Michael grabbed his unnecessary cane and made his way to the mosque.

The street was filled with police and press vans. Women from the community were wailing over their children slaughtered on British soil. The Imam Raashid Mohammad stood outside the mosque and demanded a full investigation into the senseless crime.

"The persecution and now the murder of our people can only provoke more violence," the Imam stated to the press standing near the Mosque entrance.

The Machine standing amid the crowd could sense by the religious leader's words that something was going to happen, something he must have missed during his undercover operation. The Imam was preparing the press for the bigger story. Think, Michael, what did you miss? He thought to himself. He would need to get closer to the head of the mosque. There must be a second team. I won't make that mistake again.

Ben finally made his way past the crowd into the mosque as flashing cameras and a videotaping crew added to the pandemonium. He put out his mat and began praying along with many others of the church who felt there was nothing else they could do. His next move was to find the other team of suicide assassins, and his second sense said he wouldn't have to go too far or wait too long.

Michael was angry at himself for focusing on just the young group of men. He knew better than to get tunnel vision in an operation because it could get a soldier blindsided by the unexpected. He had fixated on the young Muslim group and their belief system because his heart was trying to save them from their fate. He thought again about how young minds could be manipulated by an altered and warped belief in God. He wondered about his own faith and a church that sent countless thousands to their death during the Crusades. Michael reassured himself that when left to humans, God's plan would get distorted and misguided by man's desire for power. He immediately broadened his view of the situation and hoped that he wasn't too late to stop what could be worse than 9/11.

Chapter Five: Illusion

Back in Washington, Ted was sitting at his desk looking at his computer screen. Suddenly, it flashed a BBC report with news about the senseless murder of seven Muslim youths outside a mosque in the London district of Soho. Tess walked in with some paperwork that required her boss's signature. He didn't take his eyes off the screen, which surprised Tess because he always seemed to give her his full attention when she came into his office.

"What are you looking at?" Tess inquired.

"Seven young Muslims were just killed in front of their mosque by what the London authorities are calling a sniper attack," Ted responded as their eyes met.

Tess moved behind him to look over his shoulder to see for herself. She thought to herself, It could be Michael.

"Hey, maybe it's your guy Michael," Ted said jokingly.

Tess wasn't laughing. "You know that isn't possible, Ted, but I'm going to make some phone calls and see what other information I might be able to get from the CIA, to give us a better picture of what we're looking at, okay?"

"Sounds great, Tess." Ted wanted to kick himself for making light of her loss. "This could become an international nightmare," Ted said, changing his tone.

Tess went back to her desk and pulled up the same video feed of the murder aftermath. She watched the screen as the Imam declared that the murder could only promote more violence. Her eyes were fixed on an elderly bearded man moving toward the mosque doors just as the Imam was speaking. She froze the video and enlarged the image. Was it Michael? She looked closer and there it was, a very small beauty mark on his left earlobe. She was sure. She told him it would be the perfect place to pierce his ear if he ever thought of doing it. Tears began to flow as she breathed a sigh of relief that her love was still alive. It took her a few minutes to compose herself, and she decided not to share the information with Ted. The longer Michael was thought dead, the better his chances of staying alive…at least until I get my hands on him. She thought to herself, her anger almost palpable.

Aqeel Gabany was on the phone with the Imam of Berwick mosque. He was discussing the death of his suicide squad and the potential danger of the church being bugged by Interpol.

"I assure you, Aqeel, I have swept the building repeatedly, and there are no bugs," Raashid said.

"Well, what do you think happened?" Aqeel questioned.

"I think young boys talk too much, and some local English hate mongers must have taken the law into their own hands," the Imam answered; then went on to say, "Remember Aqeel, these English have been dealing with Irish terrorists for centuries. They have no qualms about taking the law into their own hands."

"You are probably right, but I have information about a terrorist task force of unknown size that is uncovering our plans and using deadly force. It could be them, so watch yourself." Aqeel updated the Imam. "This may actually work better for us because now it will look like a response to a senseless murder," Aqeel concluded.

“Yes, we await your command to move forward.” The Imam declared.

“Let's allow the press to report on this for a few days before we move. We'll give them the illusion that there will be no response and then boom!” Aqeel said, laughing.

The Machine had seen a few suspicious groups of men coming through the mosque, but he focused on the most obvious and vocal group. This was a big mistake not to consider multiple possibilities. He knew from his understanding of the terrorist hierarchy that the Imam was in charge. Surveillance of him would be crucial, and Michael got a sense of urgency that he would have to get information more quickly, or he would be too late to stop an act of terrorism that would make 9/11 pale in contrast. He also began to follow a man by the name of Musa, who was seen going in and out of the Imam's office before and even more frequently after the young men were killed. This proved to be just the right path to follow, and Michael told his Lord Thank you for moving him in the right direction.

Musa Abidad was from Qom, which was a small suburb of Tehran. He was an associate of Aqeel Gabany from his days after returning from college in the United States. The two met in Tehran, attending a meeting organized by Osama bin Laden about the future of Muslims after the United States' occupation of the Middle East. It was a recruiting rally to get zealots involved in the business of creating terror around the world.

Abidad was considered muscle and one who could easily be persuaded to kill himself for Allah. Aqeel liked him very much, and the two became friends, but as they were being directed into diverse levels within the terrorist organization, Aqeel was told to sever his close ties to Musa because his friend would one day be asked to give his life for the cause, and that Aqeel may be the one to send him to that destiny. Now, twelve years later, that is exactly what came to be.

Musa lived in a small flat right in the very heart of Soho, above a restaurant called Ba Shan at 24 Romilly Street, a short walking distance from the mosque. He and his friends were loud, arrogant, and very disrespectful of the landlord. They frequented the local whore houses and Gentlemen's clubs.

Michael had become well acquainted with many in the community and knew Omar Sharir, the owner of the Ba Shan restaurant, whom he called Chef out of respect for his artistry in the kitchen. The bistro was known for its Persian favorites, especially Bademjan, a Lamb stew made with tomatoes and eggplant. The chef owned the establishment for over ten years and lived in the second apartment upstairs.

Michael asked, “Chef, how long has the man been renting from you?”

“Why do you ask, Ben?” asked Omar.

“I have been thinking of moving a bit closer to the mosque. These tired old legs are beginning to give out on me. You know what I mean?” Michael said convincingly.

“I understand completely. I don't think he'll be here too much longer. I had a confrontation with him just the other day.” Omar confided in the old man.

“What happened?” Michael asked.

"He and his friends are always up half the night drinking and carrying on, and you know I'm up at the crack of dawn to get to the vegetable market to stock up for the restaurant. When I warned him about the excessive noise, he glared at me with a look that frightened me to the bone. Thank Allah, he told me yesterday he would be leaving soon. He looks dangerous to me. So, when he's gone, I will show you the place."

"I'll check back in a few days, then okay?" Ben asked.

"Sure, I'd love to rent to you," Omar said, shaking Michael's hand.

Michael turned and waved with his free hand as he hobbled down the street toward the mosque. All the while, questions and decisions were coming to the surface. How much time before the attack? How many others are there? No sleep tonight, this could go down tomorrow. Surveillance essential.

Ben made his way back to the mosque in time to perform the Isha Prayer, the evening prayer of praise to Allah. He placed his prayer rug on the ground at the rear of the mosque, symbolizing his humility, but for The Machine, it was to visualize all coming in, especially Musa and his friends. Michael didn't have to wait too long as Musa and five others walked in together and took places closest to the front of the mosque. He heard them all recite the special prayer for success.

"In the name of Allah, The Beneficent, The Merciful. I seek refuge from the accursed Satan, please accept my prayer...I seek Thy refuge from anxiety and grief, I seek Thy refuge from lack of strength and laziness, I seek Thy refuge from cowardice and niggardliness, I seek Thy refuge from being overpowered by debt and from the oppression of men. Suffice Thou me, with what is lawful. Turn away from me the things that Thou prohibit. And with Thy Grace, please keep me free from want of what is besides Thee. Amen."

This is going to happen tomorrow, he thought to himself.

When prayer was over, he watched as Musa and his friends followed the Imam into his office. Michael took this as an opportunity to set a trap. He stood outside the mosque and made an anonymous call to Scotland Yard. He told them he believed that there was a terrorist cell that was going to do something terrible the following day. He gave them the address on Romilly Street and told them to bring a bomb squad.

As the group left the mosque, he followed them to the famous Sunset Strip on Dean Street, a Gentlemen's Club that had been around since 1960. Michael's knowledge of his enemy and the past actions of the terrorists of 9/11 made it clear these boys were out for a big night before sacrificing themselves for Allah.

Michael waited until they were inside and pulled out his cell phone to fill in the authorities of their location. He thought about going in and taking them out himself, but remembered the last time when a civilian was shot by the enemy, and removed it as an option. He kept watch until a large vehicle showed up from the SO19, Britain's version of a SWAT team. His undercover operation was almost complete; there was just one last detail before he headed back to the States.

The nightlife in the area was just getting started as The Machine made his way back to the mosque. The Imam opened his door and invited Ben inside without hesitation.

"We need to talk," proclaimed the icy voice.

“What can I do for you, Benjamin?” the Imam asked.

“I need you to fill in the blanks for me,” came the response.

“I don't understand,” remarked the cleric.

“You will.” The Machine said as he pulled his hunting knife from inside his baggy pants.

“What is the meaning of this?” the religious man questioned with indignation.

“I'll ask the questions from now on,” came the response, followed by a blow that brought the cleric to the ground.

Michael shoved a handkerchief into his mouth, then ripped the cord of a nearby lamp and tied up the Imam. He placed the man on the floor and searched him for his cell phone. Once found, he pulled up recent calls and found Aqeel's number. He dialed and put it on speaker.

“Hello, Aqeel,” Michael said warmly.

“Raashid, is that you?” Aqeel asked, a bit unsure of the sound of the voice on the other end.

“No, I'm afraid your Imam will not be of any assistance to you after tonight,” came the icy voice through the line.

With that, Michael cut a finger off the religious leader, pulled the cloth from his mouth, and allowed him to get half a scream out before replacing it. This was followed by the sound of buttons being ripped off a shirt. Once the Machine exposed flesh, he carefully began to make an incision into the abdominal region. The Imam weakly moaned and briefly lost consciousness. He described to Aqeel in detail what he was doing, not leaving anything to his imagination. Within a few minutes, the Imam was disemboweled but still alive and moaning.

The Machine spoke softly into the cell phone, "Listen carefully, Aqeel."

He removed the stuffing from the Imam's mouth, raised the hunting knife well over his head, and plunged it to the hilt into the man's black heart. The holy man let out a weak scream, and his body quivered for just a moment until death overtook him.

"Did you hear that, Aqeel? That was my hunting knife, finalizing the Imam's journey to hell. Your death will not be so humane. It will be slow and methodical, and you will join your Imam very soon, because I am coming for you!"

"You are mad." Aqeel's squealing voice screamed into the phone.

A moment later, the phone went dead.

Chapter Six: The Puppet

After almost four hours, his hands were still trembling in fear as Aqeel dialed to speak to Chet Avery. Every station was broadcasting the thwarted plot to destroy the tube in England and the arrest of a group of terrorists. Chet wasted no time with insincere pleasantries but instead just filled in all the private details from Scotland Yard, receiving an anonymous lead to the apartment filled with explosives and a follow-up call detailing the whereabouts of the terrorists, which led to their capture. The information provided appeared to be so concise that Scotland Yard was sure it was an inside source from within the terrorist cell. They also indicated that the cache of explosives in their apartment was enough to demolish the London Tube subway system three times over.

Aqeel made a nervous moaning sound.

"What's wrong with you?" Chet asked, hearing the shakiness in Aqeel's voice.

"Nothing," he said. "How is our young senator doing?" Aqeel deflected, responding to his own fear.

"It would appear he is voting just as you suggested. What have you got on him?" Chet inquired.

"Our young politician is the product of a combination which includes greed, idealism, and narcissism. We carefully selected a lonely black man who lived in many various places growing up and was not inspired by patriotism and exceptionalism for the United States. Instead, we taught him that his country was not exceptional but went out of its way to try to change every government to be like its own. We assured him that their audacity needed to be curtailed by someone as brilliant as he believed himself to be. He had no real religious affiliation, which made him more pliable to accepting the Muslim faith as one that was being persecuted. Then, by dangling an outrageous amount of money and the possibility of untold power in front of his nose, he jumped at the chance and was excited to do whatever we asked of him. That Mr. Avery is the way you create the perfect puppet." Aqeel, finally recovering from his trembling, boasted through the telephone line, then added, "I'll be leaving D.C. very soon, but I will be in touch." He abruptly hung up.

Although the self-proclaimed mastermind was still shaken after hearing a man die on the phone and being threatened by unknown forces, he was very proud of what he had done so far in his plan to destroy the United States, despite the failures, which he considered small setbacks in his master plan. He sat back in his chair thinking. I studied American history very well. Lincoln warned that America could never be defeated by forces outside the United States, but that if they were not careful, they would lose everything from within. Even before our terrorist forces attacked the United States on 9/11, we had already infiltrated the American landscape by migrating into small towns all over the country. What we needed most of all was an inside man, a well-spoken minority person who was well educated and very articulate. Someone who would speak to the ideals that made America the greatest experiment in all of history. A statesman who would eloquently vow to reconnect their country with the promise of Abraham Lincoln to be a land of the people, by the people, and for the people. A man who would follow instructions without question. A pawn who, for the sake of fame and fortune, would sell out America for what he considered the greater good. A person so full of himself that nothing else mattered but what he thought, and finally someone who could be directed to do my bidding by throwing obscene amounts of money at him.

Aqeel found such a person in the heart of Harlem. Grady Morrison was from an average American family, upper middle class, whose father's job moved the family around the country, growing up never in a place long enough to develop any lasting relationships. Aqeel persuaded him that he could be quite the statesman. He pulled some strings to make sure Grady found his way into an Ivy League University financed by Muslim sources. He used his skill in controlling the weak, vulnerable mind of the young man, convincing him to major in Constitutional law. Grady went on to become involved in community organizing. His greatest ability was to produce excitement in his speeches, which found him a guest speaking spot at the Democratic Convention shortly after securing a seat in the state legislature of Indiana. His oration was moving and spoke of hope and change for all Americans. As his political star was rising, the American Press began to woo the young senator. Their objectivity was all but gone as they embraced this man for the ages. The result was an easily manipulated press that refused to vet the black pawn because they didn't want to be called racist by any negatives they might have found, and whose past was virtually ignored for the hope he projected in his speeches. A person so full of himself, he was perfect to control for a much larger plan of attack against the greatest power the world had ever known.

Yes, Aqeel praised himself. I have studied American History well, and I'll use the prophesy of one of its most respected Presidents, Abraham Lincoln, to accomplish our final goal, which is to destroy America from within, and no secret U.S. Navy SEAL force or CIA operatives will be able to stop me.

Chapter Seven: Reconnection

Michael was coming home. He no longer looked like an old Muslim man but rather a younger version of himself. His head was closely shaved bald, and he cut and trimmed his beard, leaving a goatee and mustache, which he dyed black. The fact that Michael was working out every day while he was gone made him look twenty years younger. He turned on his phone for the first time in six long months as he deplaned at Dulles. He looked down to see fifty or more calls from Tess. He wasn't quite ready to deal with her, so he dropped the phone into his coat pocket and pulled out his passport. He looked down and read his name out loud, "David Devlin."

Once outside, he hailed a cab and directed the driver to take him to the Watergate West Hotel. It was normally a half-hour drive, but the traffic was very heavy. Michael blamed the White House because the local police stopped all traffic if the President or Vice President was traveling through town. He didn't mind the ride because he was home in the country he loved.

He checked into the massive hotel, requesting a room on the fifth floor with a view of the pool. His hand slipped the desk clerk a hundred-dollar bill, assuring the guest that he would get what he wanted. Michael's thought process was that if he was cornered by authorities, the plunge down into the pool would be survivable and allow him a potentially quick departure.

"Looks like we have just what you're looking for, Mr. Devlin," the hotel clerk said as he handed Michael a pass card for room 511.

Over six months had gone by, and Michael wanted to check in on his buddy in the Philippines. He made the call and was glad to hear the voice of Chopper on the other end.

"Chopper. How can I do for you?"

"How are you, Chopper?" he asked.

"Recovering well, John, thanks for asking. Have you found a place to hang your hat for a while?"

"I just checked into the Watergate in Washington, D.C. Why?" Michael asked.

"I have a package of important goods you might need while you're there. Shall I send it?"

"Address it to David Devlin, room 511, Watergate Hotel, Washington, D.C.," Michael answered.

"That's a catchy name, John," Chopper commented.

"The real name is Michael." He confessed.

"Alright, Michael, expect a package very soon." Chopper hung up.

If he read the conversation correctly, it was a package with some tools of his trade. He arrived in town with nothing, but he and Betty were feeling a bit vulnerable. Michael looked at his phone, thinking he should make the call, but decided to wait until he got a bit more comfortable.

Once he unpacked and got settled, he again picked up his phone. He was dreading the call to Tess, which was so long overdue, but she was his only connection. He had waited too long already. He dialed. It rang twice before her voice came through the line.

"Hello, you bastard," she said angrily, recognizing the number on her cell.

"Hi, honey, I'm home," he answered her, lyrically trying to lessen the blow.

"Do you have even the slightest idea of the hell I've been going through? Just tell me why you couldn't call or at least get a message to me?" Tess wanted answers.

"I was on my way home when my inside man contacted me with information about something going down in England. Time is a luxury, Tess. You know that. I can't promise you a tomorrow, Tess, all I can do is show up occasionally for a today. So, if you come, don't come mad. I'm at the Watergate West, room 511. Do not be followed, and do me a favor, sweetheart. Bring a weapon or two, I'm a bit naked here." Michael was being as honest as he could be and hoping it would be enough for her to forgive him.

"Alright, give me an hour to stop being mad at you, and I'll bring you a few things, but if you're naked, don't get dressed." She hung up before he could say anything.

Michael looked at the cell phone and laughed. "What a girl!" He threw the phone on the bed and made his way to the bathroom for a shower and another shave after the long transatlantic flight.

Michael couldn't shake the fact that his old boss had Aqeel's number in the Philippines. What, he thought to himself, did Chet Avery have to do with a terrorist whose arms stretched around the globe? Could he be a Benedict Arnold to our country? Feeling the hot shower with fantastic water pressure made him glad he was back in the States. Tess was coming over, and Michael had butterflies in his stomach. He was getting very excited to see her again. His thoughts about Chet returned. Looks like Chet and I will be having a conversation very soon. I need answers.

Across town, Tess was doing the same thing as Michael. She had removed her work clothes and jumped into the shower. Her body and soul were in an excited state. She looked down and noticed her hands were shaking, as her thoughts of the last time they had touched each other raced through her mind. Part of her wanted to be mad at him, but her love for him was overpowering everything else. She quickly rinsed off the soap and exited the shower. She only towel-dried her hair, then put on some makeup and quickly got dressed. She went to her safe and brought out two handguns with multiple clips, placed them into her purse, took one last look at herself in the mirror by her door, then hurried out.

On her way to her car, she thought about what he said. His inside man, when did that happen? It was a question she would want to get answered in a little while. Her mind raced. What if he doesn't want this anymore? I'm so angry at him I could scream. Keep it together, Tess, for thirty minutes, and you'll see him; then the answers will come.

The ride over was sporatic to ensure she was not being followed, but she wondered why he thought she might be. She knew there were times not to question but follow instructions. This was one of those times. She left the window open, and the warm Washington breeze dried her hair as she drove. She stopped into the women's bathroom near the lobby to inspect and make some final adjustments to her hair.

Michael heard the knock on the door just after he had splashed some cologne on his face. He only managed to get his Levi's on when he made it to the door. He looked through the peephole to see who it was. When he saw it was Tess, his stomach started to do flips. He opened the door. The two lovers could only stare at each other. Tess almost didn't recognize him, and in that first moment, time seemed to stand still. An instant later, Tess was in his arms.

She thought she would never touch him again. She needed to just embrace him. Her emotions were undone as she began to sob uncontrollably. Michael put his large right hand on her head, consoling her as he shut the door with the other; then he gently embraced her. She cried for a long time. Michael knew to give her a chance to work through so many emotions. He needed to work through his own overwhelming feelings. He thought about how much he loved her, how much he had missed her touch, how good she felt in his arms, and how their future was already doomed by the path he had chosen. As her smell filled his nostrils, everything else began to melt away.

Finally, she looked up with teary eyes and began hitting his hairy chest with her fists. "How could you let me think you were dead?" She was venting all the anger and frustration she had for his not calling her. Even though she was sure it was him trying to protect her from the pain she would experience, regardless of whether she was in or out of the loop. He didn't answer her; instead, he stood motionless, taking the attack; her onslaught continued for a brief time until it was replaced with her open hands on his chest. She was emotionally spent, and although she wanted to scream at him, she knew the last thing he needed in the middle of a war was a complaining sweetheart. Instead, she began to kiss his chest. She couldn't help but whimper as her lips delivered wet kisses. Michael understood and responded with kisses to her head. Their lips finally met, mixed with the wetness of her tears. She was almost lost.

"It won't happen again, Tess. I promise." Michael said softly. His hands reached down, cupped her cheeks until they were face to face, and he used his thumbs to wipe away her tears. His lips touched hers so tenderly that Tess felt electricity move between them. She stopped crying, placed her hands on his face, and pressed her lips firmly against his; her need to have him was being sent in her kisses. The message was received, and Michael scooped her up in his arms and laid her gently on the bed. He moved over her and kissed her face all over quickly. She giggled, but just for a second. His intentions became clear. His fingers unbuttoned her blouse while his lips were making their way down her stomach, and she quivered, knowing where he was going and what she would be feeling in a second or two. She wasn't disappointed as he devoured her. She climaxed and then climaxed again, her body convulsing in pure ecstasy. Michael kissed his way back up her beautiful body, pausing to give each of her breasts full attention. Her nipples were swollen from the arousal, and she could barely catch her breath. She used her hands to gently guide him back to her lips. She wanted to feel him inside her. A second later, she got her wish. Their rhythm was slow. They stared at each other, and both began to shed tears as they came to the realization of how precious each second was in their existence with one another. Their expression of love was complete, each giving a hundred percent to the other. Their breathing slowed just briefly as he continued to move gently back and forth within her. His manhood remained firm as he moved. They made love for almost two hours. Michael used his fingers to memorize every inch of her with Tess doing the same, neither one wanting it to end. Even though exhaustion overcame them, they remained entangled.

Tess had learned over the years about the power of prayer through Michael and his beliefs. He had told her that in one's desperation, turn to God because if it fits into His plan, prayers are answered positively. She lay there in the darkness as Michael slept, and she asked God for more tomorrows and for a happy ending. She also knew if God's plan didn't include tomorrows, there might be no answer at all. That possibility brought silent tears dropping onto the pillow until sleep found her.

Michael woke first. He looked at her sleeping, her hair stuck to her face from so much perspiration. He used his fingers to fix her hair. It made her wake.

"I don't want this to ever end," Michael said as he looked at her beautiful face in the morning.

"I think you love me, Michael," she responded as she rubbed the dried tears from her eyes.

"I do love you, Tess, more than I thought possible."

They lied there, propped up on their arms, looking at each other in bed. They stared at each other for a long time without a word spoken. The room smelled of love. They gently touched each other to make sure they weren't dreaming.

After the longest time, his voice finally broke the silence. "I'm probably not going to survive this war, what can one man do…" Tess put her finger to his lips, cutting him off. She replaced her finger with her lips, and he responded in silence. They moved together into one being. A syncopated rhythm ensued. He knew she understood the reality of their situation, and her movement told him clearly that she didn't want to do anything but live for the few moments they had without thinking about tomorrow. He would comply, giving her every bit of himself, mind, body, and soul.

Time moved too quickly for the two lovers who had gotten very little sleep. Michael called room service and ordered breakfast for two with an extra coffee. Hearing him, Tess rolled over and looked at the bedside clock, which showed nine thirty. She dialed Ted on his cell. When she didn't get an answer, she left him a message. "This is Tess. I'm taking a sick day, totally exhausted, call me on my cell if anything crazy happens, otherwise I'll see you tomorrow." She dropped the phone on the floor on her side of the bed, then reached for Michael. He found her reaching hand with his own and laced his fingers with hers. He kissed the back of her hand and continued kissing his way up her arm.

"You're giving me goose bumps," she said, showing him her arm.

"Aren't you sick of me yet?" he inquired seriously.

"Michael, I have been in love with you for so long. This past year, I found that I love you even more than I thought I could and, given our situation, way more than I wanted to."

"Same here, kid. You know how I feel about God and country. I am learning that He has a plan for all of us. The timing of what we have seems like it sucks, but maybe not according to Him." He said knowingly, pointing his finger towards Heaven.

There was a knock on the door and a voice calling, "Room Service."

Tess grabbed Michael's shirt and quickly buttoned it up for modesty. Michael went to the door and signed the bill. "I'll leave the cart outside when we're done, okay?" Michael asked and slipped the waiter a twenty. The waiter nodded and left. Michael brought the cart in.

Michael changed the subject after sipping his coffee. "This country of ours is headed for a lot of trouble, because what's happening in England has already started here with the terrorists' infiltration into the population. That means their agenda becomes easier to accomplish. We have politicians who are trying so hard to be sensitive to Muslims that they are turning their heads to a potential threat from the radical jihadists who hide in their midst. Geez, Tess, in Galveston, the head of the hospital was one of them. Only God knows where else they are being placed."

"Honey, eat your breakfast, you're not going into battle today. Today you're mine." Tess said with authority.

"Yes, dear, but I'm afraid I've got a few things I need to do," Michael said, realizing that he had gotten on his soapbox. He quickly ate a few pieces of bacon and drank his coffee, then disappeared into the bathroom. After a few minutes, Tess heard the shower start, and she took off Michael's shirt, laid it on the bed, entered the bathroom, and slipped into the shower behind him.

"Let me get your back." She purred.

Michael handed her the hotel soap and a washcloth, and she proceeded to wash his back. She told him she could feel all his muscles as she scrubbed. When she was sure she had done an excellent job, she turned him around so the shower could rinse him off. She looked down and saw his manhood coming to life. Tess wanted to show her affection in the most intimate way, and Michael was too overwhelmed by her to say no.

Afterwards, they dried off and went back to bed naked. Michael needed some recovery time, so he brought up some questions concerning Avery that had been bugging him for some time. He wanted Tess to help him make sense of it.

"Why would Chet have the phone number of Aqeel Gabany?"

"Maybe he's been providing information to Chet." Tess pondered.

"If that were the case, you and I would have been notified," Michael told her with assurance.

"I don't know. Maybe Aqeel is just a government diplomat for Iran that Chet has been meeting with?"

"Maybe, but this guy is pulling the strings of terrorist cells all around the world. Do you think our people have a file on him? I'm going to have a talk with Chet very soon, and if I get information that he is somehow involved in any way with Aqeel, Chet is going to die a horrible death." Michael's alter ego was coming through, and Tess got frightened.

"Michael, there has to be a logical reason why he has the number," she rationalized.

"Tell me what reason?" he barked back.

"Michael, you wouldn't really hurt him, would you?" Tess couldn't grasp the significance of his statement.

"Tess, over three thousand citizens, most of them innocent civilians, died that day in New York. If Chet was involved in any way that led to those deaths…" Michael was cut off by Tess.

"If that's the case, just turn him over to the justice department."

"I'll have a conversation with him, and we'll see where it takes us. Fair enough?"

"Okay," she replied.

The desire of the two lovers was replaced with the job at hand, and both became aware that it needed to take priority. Michael had to begin surveillance of his old boss, and Tess needed to be in a place where she could provide her man with any information that might come out of her office. She called in and asked to speak to Ted Hobson. Once on the line, she told her boss that she would be in after all. She told him she thought it was a migraine, but it went away.

The lovers exchanged glances with each other as they put on their clothes. Michael took a last sip of coffee and asked Tess for a ride to the closest rental car place. She nodded as she picked up her purse and slipped into her heels.

Tess reached into her bag. "I almost forgot, here is the 380 with a few extra clips you requested. I threw in a silencer."

"I wasn't that specific, but thanks for remembering my favorite weapon," Michael said politely.

Tess leaned into him and kissed him with both hands on his face. "I'll check to see if there is a file for Gabany." She continued to squeeze his face with both hands. "God, I love you."

Tess turned her car onto New Hampshire Ave. NW, sped a quick three blocks, made a left onto Pennsylvania Ave., drove another few minutes to M Street, and pulled into the driveway of the Zipcar rental office. They didn't talk during the five-minute drive, but before Michael got out of the car, he leaned over and gave her a long kiss. She told him to keep his phone on. He assured her he would and exited the car.

As Tess drove away, her mind was swirling through her past. The woman she had become didn't happen overnight. It was an accumulation of experiences from growing up in Brooklyn to meeting Michael Angelino and a lot of stuff in between.

Tess was raised by her mother Eufemia and her father Salvatore, a conductor for the subway, during a time of internal decline caused by the closing of the Navy shipyard in 1966, with even basic services decreased due to infrastructure decay. Gas prices and shortages made everyday living a struggle for the Lamia family. Eufemia worked in her brother's delicatessen. She made sure there was plenty of food on the dining room table. It made them all feel like everything was going to be okay. Tess went to the Brathwaite School, which was started by concerned parents after the diocese run by Bishop Francis Mugaverose decided to close several schools due to a lack of sufficient funding.

By the mid-seventies, gangs sprang up, and organized crime was putting tariffs on local businesses for protection. This resulted in Brooklyn getting the reputation for the highest murder rate in the country. Tess's father was one of the victims in 1976, when he was shot by a stray bullet fired near the train, while he was pulling into the subway station in Flatbush.

After her father's death and her mother describing gangsters coming in weekly to the deli for their protection money, Tess became interested in what she could do to exact change. She studied criminal justice at Kingsborough Junior College. She went to school during the day and worked the dinner shift at the deli in the evenings, which didn't leave her any time for romance. After getting her AA degree, she went on to NYU for her Bachelor of Science degree in psychology, and it was there that she met Lance Barber, who was majoring in criminal justice. They dated all through most of her last two years of college.

Those years at NYU were intense, and she minored in physical education. Tess knew that as a woman going into law enforcement, she would encounter peers who would challenge her physical abilities to do the job and perps who might consider resisting arrest because she was a woman. She became the best in hand-to-hand combat and could run faster than most of the men. This eventually became too much of a problem for Lance, who, although a good man, was intimidated by her superior abilities. He broke up with her just before graduation.

Tess didn't let the break-up stop her. She joined the NYPD and put in two very rough years, dealing with fellow officers who were male chauvinists. They railed at her all the time, but she dealt with it by being the best shot on the shooting range and by proving herself in the field against criminals twice her size. She spent her off-hours studying for her master's in finance.

After a grueling entrance exam, which was both written and physical, Tess Lamia found herself in Quantico, Virginia, forty miles south of Washington D.C., at the FBI Academy, which is proudly called the West Point of Law Enforcement. The Academy was opened in 1972 and grew out of a need for agents to be better equipped to handle weapons. The twenty-one-week training was intensive both mentally and physically.

It was there she met a visiting guest speaker by the name of Agent Michael Angelino. This distinguished man with a deep brown beard and slightly balding spoke to her class about combating the threat of public corruption around the borders, specifically our neighbor to the south. His emphasis was on drug trafficking and the potential of terrorism with such insecure borders. Tess went up after his talk to introduce herself and to thank him for the real on-the-job look at the dangers that exist. Unbeknownst to Tess, Michael made a mental note of her name. Her excitement was diminished when she noticed the ring on his finger.

She dated sporadically and even allowed herself to be intimate a few times in an effort to find happiness, but nothing ever came of it. So, after repeated intense relationships that led nowhere, she made it her goal to become the very best in the field and to eventually find herself in a senior investigative position. For five years, she worked as a field agent, receiving the FBI Medal for Meritorious Achievement for rescuing a civilian who was shot by criminals attempting to rob a bank in Kansas. While under fire, she made her way to the wounded lady, was able to apply a pressure dressing on the wound, and dragged the woman to a safe place. Once the criminals were dealt with, she stayed with the woman until the paramedics arrived.

When the position came up to work for the Joint Terrorism Task Force in Washington, D.C., in 1990, she applied. At the interview, she was surprised to see Agent Angelino in attendance, looking older with a bit of gray in his beard and a lot less hair on his head, but still very handsome and charismatic. He reviewed her service record and rubbed his beard as he did so. Tess was so nervous because the room was silent for a long time, it seemed. In fact, it was just a minute or two, but it felt longer. Finally, he looked up from the file and asked, “Will it bother you to do most of your work behind a desk?”

Tess remained silent, watching his face, his blue-gray eyes seeming to pierce hers. “I believe my clinical skills match my physical ability, sir. So, no, sir, I don’t believe it will bother me.”

“Good, looks like you’re an excellent shot. Do you practice a lot?” Michael asked with what appeared to be a small smile.

"At least once a week, sir," Tess answered.

"Good, because there may come a time we'll be in the field together and I'd like my partner to be able to cover my ass if under fire." Michael's smile was obvious.

"Sir, may I ask a question?" She asked, and Michael nodded in the affirmative. "How good a shot are you?"

"I think I can assure you, you'll be safe with me. Thanks, Miss Lamia, we'll be in touch."

"Thank you, gentlemen." She stood to leave the room.

Michael leaned over to the other agent, said something she couldn't hear, then said as she was leaving, "You'll start on Monday, okay?"

She turned with a big smile. "Yes, sir."

"Oh yeah, just call me Michael." He replied.

"Okay, sir…Michael." Tess stuttered and walked from the room, beaming.

Now that man was her lover and friend, and he was going to investigate their old superior about his loyalty to America, a loyalty that was paramount to Michael, and for that reason, she was afraid of what might happen.

Chapter Eight: Discovery

Once David Devlin signed the papers for his rental car, he made his way over to the home of Chet Avery. It was about an hour drive on the 50 freeway east to the small bay community of Edgewater. Michael was there a few times during his tenure at the Pentagon, but Avery was a pretty private person, single and kept to himself. This made Michael's sixth sense go into hyperdrive, and if he had secrets, Michael might find answers in his home.

The road forced him to think, and sometimes that wasn't always a good thing. On the way, Michael and God had a conversation about Tess and their relationship. His feelings for Tess were getting more serious than he ever expected, and that made him think that what they were doing wasn't according to God's plan. What am I supposed to do about it? Am I in the middle of a war? He questioned himself. He waited for an answer, and it came quickly. Trust in the Lord in all things. The phase kept coming to him. He needed to get right with God. Michael did most of the talking. Okay, you know how much I love her. Yes, I know the sex thing doesn't work for you, but I don't know about tomorrow. She'll probably be a widow in a very short time. Is that what you want for her? The odds against me are overwhelming. Michael thought to himself. I know what you said. "Therefore, do not worry about tomorrow, for tomorrow will worry about itself. Each day has enough trouble of its own. He looked to Heaven briefly, "You're always right, aren't you?"

Michael arrived in Chet's neighborhood and parked his car down the suburban street from the well-manicured house. He walked up the driveway of the white two-story home. Unsure if there was a security system, Michael went to the electrical panel and shut the main switch off. He broke the rear entrance window pane and slipped his hand in to unlock the door. His experience had taught him to start in the most obvious place, which for someone hiding something would be either the office or their bedroom.

Michael made his way upstairs and into the master bedroom, which appeared smaller than he would have imagined. On the far side of the room, across from the bed, was a built-in bookcase. He looked closer at the hardwood floor and noticed a very tiny hint of a mark that could suggest that the bookcase might be the entrance to another room. He ran his fingers on the inside edge of the bookcase until his fingers found a button, which he depressed. The bookcase clicked forward toward him. He made his way inside. There was a twin bed with handcuffs hanging from each bedpost. A video camera was also set up facing the bed. Michael began to get a sick feeling in his stomach. He moved beyond the camera to a shelf filled with VHS video tapes. The tapes were dated with male and female names on each tape. The dates went back almost ten years. Michael knew that he needed to see what Chet was up to, so he pulled a tape from the shelf, opened the plastic cover, and inserted the video into the camera. He pressed play and waited.

Suddenly, there was a very young girl on the bed, she was naked and in handcuffs. She appeared to be drugged. Her head was shifting from one side to the other. The man Michael answered to for so many years came into view wearing a mask. He began at first to fondle the young girl, bringing on arousal. Then he bit her nipple so hard it bled. The young girl began to cry. This caused the masked attacker to get an erection. He removed one of the handcuffs, flipped her over, then reattached them on the same bed post, then he put some petroleum jelly on her anus. The assault was vicious. Michael had seen enough. He wanted to kill the monster on the screen. He pressed the stop button, then the rewind button until it came to a halt. He replaced the video in its spot and retraced his steps until he was outside. Once back in his car, he headed down the road, and he pulled out his cell to contact his old boss.

"Chet Avery, can I help you?" Chet announced in his customary way.

"Chet, tell me how you know Aqeel Gabany," came an icy voice.

"Michael…Michael, is that you?" he questioned in shock.

"Answer the question, Avery!" the voice got slightly louder.

"Michael, you need to turn yourself in to the FBI. They think you may be involved in the murders in Galveston and Mexico City."

"It was me, Chet, but right now I'm thinking of how to kill you. I've been at your house and your secret room."

"Oh, Michael. It's not what you think." Chet pleaded for understanding.

"It's worse, Avery. You have a proclivity to inflict pain on young boys and girls. I found the tapes." Michael yelled into the cell phone.

"I have a terrible problem, Michael, and this man, Gabany, found out about it and has been blackmailing me for information. Oh, my God! Michael, I'm so sorry! He threatened to expose me." Avery admitted, sobbing into the phone.

"Don't mention God, Chet. I'm giving you two hours to turn yourself in before I am forced to act on my own, and you don't want that, Chet. You know what I'm capable of. I'm sure you've read the reports on my kills. You can thank Tess for the time, Chet. Use it wisely." Michael warned his old boss, then hung up.

Michael had barely finished the call when another call was coming through. It was his informant, Mansoor. Michael hesitated to answer the call. If he didn't, it could mean more time with Tess, sleeping in a bed one more night without an agenda, or maybe to get back a little piece of the life he had lost. He took the call.

"Where are you?" he asked without pleasantry.

"I am calling from my new office in Tehran." Mansoor declared.

"Sounds like a promotion," Michael said in a monotone voice.

"It is because of you. I am considered a hero without a finger," the informant said proudly.

"Did you ever think they might be watching you to see if you have turned on them? Mansoor, get your head out of your ass and call me from an outside line." Michael hung up the phone.

The seasoned soldier shook his head in disbelief at how naïve these new-age terrorists were. What the hell was he thinking? Suddenly, the phone rang again.

"Where are you now?"

"Safe place, many thanks, boss," Mansoor responded.

"What have you got for me?" his new boss asked.

"There will be another air attack this time in Chicago. The target is the Sears Building. Two six-man teams will be going out of JFK. One will be heading for Los Angeles, California, the other for Phoenix, Arizona. Their mission is to take control of the aircraft after it has taken off and fly the planes into the building. They are instructed to take out another large skyscraper if they see that the first target has already been hit. They have been living in New York for the past twelve weeks in Bay Ridge. I do not have all their names, but team one is headed by Ayman Zawahiri, who was responsible for the attacks in Kenya. The other team leader is Saif al-Adel. This one is a monster who hates everything American and attacked your embassy in Iran. These two groups are zealots who are more than happy to sacrifice themselves for their holy war against all infidels." Mansoor finished.

"What's the timetable?" Michael asked.

"It will be Eid al-Adha, the festival of sacrifice at the end of Hajj, the annual pilgrimage to Mecca," Mansoor replied.

"That's just a month away. I had better get started." Michael said.

He needed clarification on something he just heard. "Funny, Mansoor, earlier you used the word their instead of our. What's going on with your research? You haven't been reading the Bible, have you?" he asked, almost laughing.

"I have a boss, mostly the New Testament, especially the words in red. I'm very confused with my own faith because in the Quran it corroborates that Jesus was born to a virgin, was sinless, performed miracles, and was superior to other prophets. Yet, Islam teaches that Jesus was no more than a prophet.

"Read the prophecies that were written a thousand years before Christ was born. In them is a detailed description of Jesus, the one and only Son of God. The truth will come to you. Use the mind God gave you to find the truth." Michael said to encourage him.

"How can Jesus be only a prophet if he is without sin, since man in his very nature is sinful. Christ, if sinless must be perfect. He must be perfect and sinless, or he could not be the sacrifice for the sins of man. In your gospels, Jesus says very clearly that He and the Father are one and the same. Even after almost being beaten to death when asked by the high priest, Caiaphas, Are you the Christ, the Son of the Blessed? Jesus said, I am, and you will see the Son of Man seated at the right hand of Power. Isn't that blasphemy? If it is, why do the Muslims and the Jews hold Jesus in such high regard?"

"You're asking the right questions, Mansoor, but the journey to the truth must be taken by your desire for the truth despite what you have been taught to memorize," Michael assured him.

"If I survive the next encounter, perhaps we can discuss this further," Michael told his informant.

"I would like that a lot, boss." Mansoor barely got the words out when the phone went dead.

***

Michael was on the Maryland 214 when his phone rang again. This time it was Tess. He wasn't prepared to give her the sad news that he must leave again for New York and another potential battlefield. He pressed the answer button on his phone.

"Hello, young lady," Michael said cheerfully.

"Were you responsible in any way?" Her voice was emotional.

"What are we talking about?" Michael asked.

"Where are you?" She demanded to know.

"I'm just coming into DC." He responded.

"Chet is dead. His neighbor called the fire department when he saw smoke coming from the upstairs bedroom. When they arrived, they found a note next to his body that only said I'm sorry. Michael, they said, had his brains blown out from a shot through his mouth. The question is, did he do it or did you?"

"I promise I had nothing to do with it. I found out he was being blackmailed by Aqeel for something he had a problem with, and I told him he needed to resolve it before I did. It would appear he chose the former." Michael said, revealing as little as possible.

"The police are coming by to ask some questions. Is there anything I need to know?"

"No," came the response, followed by, Will I see you tonight?"

"I don't know, this could be a mess today. I'll try to be there as soon as possible." Tess answered, feeling uncomfortable with the way the conversation had gone.

"Okay, see you in a bit." He hung up before she could say anything else.

Michael was walking through the lobby of his hotel when the hotel manager approached him.

"Mr. Devlin, we have a package for you that arrived today. Shall we send it up, sir?"

"Please. Any messages?" Michael asked, not expecting any.

"No, sir, just the package," the manager answered.

"Okay." Michael nodded and headed for the elevator.

He just pulled his shoes off when there was a knock at the door. He grabbed the 380 and prepared for the worst out of habit. The bell boy announced he had a package for Mr. Devlin. Michael placed his weapon on the counter in the bathroom near the door of the room and opened the door, so the bellhop could push the cart carrying the package into the room. It was very heavy, so Michael placed it on the bed and pulled a twenty out of his pocket to give to the attendant. The young man enthusiastically said thank you at least three times before Michael could shut the door.

He pulled out the key of his rental car and used it like a knife on the box. Everything inside the package was wrapped in bubble wrap and white towels. As Michael went through the contents, he was particularly pleased to see the black Beretta 9mm with a five-inch barrel, which he got from Mansoor's hotel room. Chopper added five clips loaded and ready for action. He also put in an MK. 17 SCAR-H is a Belgium-made NATO assault weapon for urban warfare. This gem of a weapon was capable of unleashing 600 rounds per minute, and Chopper had twenty fully loaded 30-round magazines packed nicely in the box. The note from his friend read, Michael, if you need anything ever, just ask which includes a helicopter pilot. Your friend forever, Chopper.

Chapter Nine: Accoutrement

The Sears Tower was the largest building in the world for over twenty-five years. Built in the heart of Chicago in 1973, this structure is so tall that on a sunny day, from the observation deck, they say you can see the curvature of the Earth. With over 3.8 million square feet of office space, this building employed over 10,000 people. Because of its unique construction, it was designed structurally with nine tubes that go all the way to the 50th floor, seven continue to the 66th floor, five to the 90th floor, and the remaining three to the 108th floor. Experts indicate it would not tolerate a terrorist attack like 9/11 as well as the Twin Towers did, and would be reduced to rubble in a much shorter time, causing more human loss of life.

It's just the information Aqeel wanted when picking his next target in his people's jihad against the United States. He returned to Iran after the threatening call from the unknown American. So, when he received instructions on another plane attack, his only real decision was to see who out of his many expendable soldiers would be chosen to carry out their plan. There were two that he was sure he could count on.

***

Ayman Zawahiri was almost thirty-five years old when the call to action came from Aqeel Gabany. He was a small man with the syndrome to match. Ayman was lying low after his attack on the American Embassy in Kenya, where thirteen foreign civilians were killed. Without an American death, he felt humiliated and would do anything to change his pitiful resume. His counterpart, Saif al-Adel, was younger and much more radical in his desire to create large-scale death to America. A zealot to the Jihad, Saif had no qualms about inflicting pain on other humans. After bombing the embassy in Iran and killing three Marines, he tried to behead the fallen soldiers, but was stopped by a bullet to his right leg from their remaining forces. Saif had a visible limp because of the encounter, a constant reminder for him that there was more to do.

The two team leaders could pick their crew of five soldiers and then begin the training necessary to accomplish their mission. Gabany knew that after 9/11, getting pilot training was not going to happen in the United States, but Iran was more than happy to give its soldiers training in the takeover of an American commercial airliner. Special carry-on luggage was made with surgical steel blades inserted along the bag frame to go unnoticed by the relatively under-trained TSA agents. Each soldier was equally equipped in case any one of the others was incapacitated or killed during the hijacking. After their training, the two groups were told not to have any contact with the other team once they began the final preparation in New York. Each team would be traveling in groups of two or three to other states on a regular basis to determine if they were being observed by any authorities. The groups were in the field for five months and were living large as they prepared for their final flight. The jihadists were partaking nightly of the women of the West, getting lap dances and more as their allowance permitted, ever aware that within thirty days their lives would be over.

***

Michael was a bit angry at the way the conversation had gone with Tess. It was something that needed to be resolved before he was en route to New York. He had already secured his weapons, including the MK. 17 SCAR-H, a Belgium-made NATO assault weapon, and the 9mm Beretta. Michael was getting to know the weapon, so it would feel like a part of him in battle, and he liked the way it felt in his hand. There was a light knock on the door. He placed the Beretta inside his coat, which was hanging on a chair by the entrance.

"Hello," was all he said as Tess brought her lips to his. She could sense something was wrong. She dropped her purse on the floor and said knowingly, "I think we need to talk."

Michael started. "You need to hear this from me one time only so there can be no misunderstanding." Michael paused to read the expression on her face as she sat down on the bed. It was the same face of the young woman wanting to learn from her boss not that long ago.

"I am engaged in a war. It is very important to know who the allies are and who the enemy is, and if I find that someone I trusted is the enemy, I will kill them. The only thing I'm unsure of is how I will kill them. I might torture them to death, or I might just put a bullet between their eyes. It cannot be emotional or sentimental. Are we clear?"

Tess just nodded.

"If tomorrow I found out that your mother was in collusion with the jihadists, I would kill her dead." He waited for a response, but she sat quietly and listened. "Tess, this isn't some territorial skirmish that can be resolved after some negotiations. This is a war to the death, theirs or ours. These people would cut your beautiful head off without giving it a second thought, and to win, we must be able to do the same. Forget the Geneva Convention and the rules of engagement. If you have an opportunity to kill them, you kill them and don't think about the political ramifications, just kill them.

There can be no prisoners, only coffins in this kind of war, and if God is with us, the coffins will be theirs."

Tess began to say Chet's name when Michael cut her off.

"Chet turned his back on his country to protect himself from exposure to his perverted life, but I won't always have time to explain why I kill someone that you might think is on our side. You can't second-guess me. You need to know that I only kill bad guys, and so far, I'm batting a thousand, but I will deal with God if potential collateral damage occurs, and based on the way this war is going, it's probably just a matter of time."

Tess stood up and gently put her arms around his neck. She looked deep into his blue-grey eyes and said, "I'm sorry." She pulled him close and kissed him softly on his lips. Michael kissed her back. All the confusion was resolved, and all that was left were two people who were intensely in love.

Button after button slowly came undone until their clothes fell to the floor. Once naked, they began to ravage one another. Soft nibbles and pulled nipples took her to that special place where her mind became lost in a cloud of electrical impulses that were firing deep between her legs. Michael wasn't satisfied with her having one or two orgasms, and through the course of their love, he had discovered those key areas that sent her reeling. He began to kiss every part of her body, not leaving any nook or cranny untouched. She had never been loved so completely and started to giggle as he found more uncharted parts previously ignored. She swooned over all his attention and resolved to just let him have his way with her. Their intimacy was hot, powerful, and passionate as sweat poured from both. Michael thrust into her harder than he had before until he climaxed. A few minutes later, they lied next to each other, faces flushed and chuckling that they had become totally lost in the moment.

Michael, still naked, walked over and picked up the phone to order room service. “Two steaks, salad with balsamic vinaigrette, sourdough rolls, and New York-style cheesecake. Oh yeah, how about a nice bottle of your best Merlot? Thanks.” He hung up the phone.

He turned to Tess, who was biting the edge of the sheets as she admired her amazing lover with a devilish smile. “Hungry?”

“I am,” she said, smiling.

“Good, we have about half an hour before the food arrives.”

“What do you have in mind, stud?” she questioned seductively.

“Bad news, I’ll be leaving in a few days for New York,” Michael answered.

“What’s going on?” she asked, sitting up and a bit confused.

“It’s another terror attack in the works.” He responded.

Tess looked stunned. “I haven’t heard a word from either the CIA or the FBI about any chatter, and they’ve been really good at keeping me in the loop.”

“I think the terrorists are getting smarter about the way they are conducting this war. Intel is going to have to get better if we don’t want more buildings being destroyed.” Michael warned her.

“Is that what their plan is to bring down another building in New York? Oh, my God, the Empire State building?” she gasped after the question left her lips.

"No, it's the Sears Tower in Chicago, and there are two teams involved. So far, all I have in detail is that they are residing in Bay Ridge and that they have been there for about twelve weeks."

"If they hit that building with a commercial airliner, we'll lose at least three times the casualties we did on 9/11," Tess said with authority.

Michael looked at her and staggered at the statement. Tess could see it in his eyes and continued, "Ted had our task force staff get the structural plans for almost every key building in our busiest major cities. It included Chicago, Los Angeles, San Francisco, Dallas, and of course, New York."

"What were his recommendations?" Michael asked.

"It was concluded by our statisticians that it was highly unlikely that the terrorists would attempt a repeat of 9/11. However, I was shocked to read the structural limits of the buildings evaluated, with the Sears Tower as the one to cause the most damage in the shortest amount of time, but because of their report, our statisticians concluded it was more likely they would attempt an attack on our military installations.

"Looks like your stat guys got it wrong," Michael said as a matter of fact.

"How good is your source?" she inquired.

"Let's just say his very life and that of his family depend on it," Michael answered her confidently.

A moment later, the door tapped gently, followed by "Room Service!" Michael threw on his jeans, and Tess arranged herself modestly under the covers. Michael opened the door, slipped the young man a twenty, and took the trays off the cart. "Thanks, we won't need anything else." The orderly glanced at Tess on the bed, smiled at Michael, and looked down at a twenty placed in his hand. He nodded approvingly, said thank you, and closed the door.

Tess lost the covers, reached over, grabbed Michael's T-shirt, and put it on; then she grabbed her plate off the tray. Michael uncorked the wine and poured two glasses. He smelled the wine in his glass and then took a tiny sip and sloshed it around in his mouth. He turned to her and said, "I think you'll like this."

They continued the conversation where they left off, with Tess wanting to know exactly when he would be leaving. He filled in all the details he had to give her. After dinner and killing the wine, Michael put a piece of cheesecake on a fork and moved it toward Tess's mouth. He quickly replaced the empty fork with his mouth, and the two shared the cheesecake bite. What followed was passionate. Michael pulled Tess close to him and pulled off the shirt that covered her naked breasts. He couldn't get close enough to her, and knowing that before very long he would be gone again, he made the most of their time together. Something beautiful was happening between them. It transcended the physical. He could feel himself melding with her, not only in body but in spirit. He found himself getting emotional as they were locked in a passionate embrace. He watched her face as they moved together; her eyes were closed. When she opened them and their eyes met, both began to tear. They stayed that way throughout the encounter, and when they were done. They began to sob openly. She wanted to beg him to stay, but knew she couldn't, and he, because he was loving her with the same intensity as he had loved Elizabeth.

Late into the night, somewhere between midnight and three, they lied together, still struggling to stay awake. Michael told her very softly, "I want to memorize every inch of you, every tiny detail, and every scar and everything that makes you…you."

"I love you, Michael Angelino." tears falling from her eyes.

Tess woke to the smell of fresh-brewed coffee the following morning and two loving blue-gray eyes looking down on her. She smiled at her hero and asked, "What time is it?"

"5:30ish," he said, followed by a soft kiss on her lips.

"Why so early?" she asked, slightly confused.

"I thought you might need to get home to change, and I'm guessing that the office will want to see you, as word of Chet's death makes it through the hallways."

"You're a genius," Tess responded as she jumped out of the bed and made her way into the bathroom. She came out a few minutes later wearing only his T-shirt, pulling it down to cover herself shyly. "How many days before you leave me again?"

"A few," was all he could muster.

"Okay then, I'll try to make my office hours shorter until you leave."

"That sounds workable for me," Michael assured her.

"I'm gonna take a shower before I leave."

"Me casa e su casa," Michael said in his best Spanish.

Tess giggled and closed the door.

***

Tess arrived at the Pentagon at seven and was at her desk when Ted Hobson arrived a few minutes before eight. He peeked into her office. “Guess you heard about Chet.”

“He was a great guy, but I didn’t know him well enough outside of work. I don’t know what would make him take his own life,” she admitted to her boss.

“I don’t know either, but the White House wants this to go away as quickly as possible. I have been asked to take Chet’s position. I told them I would if I could have you take over the Terrorist task force. They agreed. Congratulations, Tess.” Ted said in a matter-of-fact way and left her to think about what he just told her.

Tess sat in her office, staring at the wall and thinking about how this might be just the right place for her to help the man she loved. Her first order of business was to investigate the death of her old boss, Chet Avery, to find out if he or his office had somehow been compromised. She, of course, already knew the answer to that, but she wanted to create misdirection away from any discussion or sightings of Michael Angelino, who was still a person of interest regarding the murders in Texas, the slaughter in Mexico City, and the chaos in the Philippines.

Chapter Ten: Extremists

New York after 9/11 was not the friendliest place for Middle Eastern men. Aqeel must have known that in advance when he chose his two suicide leaders, because the one thing these two men had in common was charisma. Saif and Ayman were liked by everyone, and that made blending into the largest melting pot known as New York just a little bit easier. The two chose cohorts who fit their personalities, respectively. The two teams were set in Iran, except for Robert Ellis, who was an American. Aqeel passed his photo around the table so they could identify him when they arrived in the United States. Once they arrived, the men went out of their way to be great neighbors to their corresponding apartment complexes. Robert Ellis joined Saif's team and took up residence with them.

Saif and his five team members lived in a Brooklyn Apartment known as The Ridge. They had a three-bedroom residence with two in each room. There was a computer in the living room where each member of the team was required to devote at least two hours a day to the pilot simulator program. Saif al-Adel was the wild card within the terrorist organization. He didn't have a beard and could pass as a model for GQ magazine. He was also a self-serving individual who wanted things done his way, regardless of the orders given. Aqeel was glad to put Saif on this mission because the result was that he would no longer have to deal with him. Saif chose not to work and made sure all his men were getting trained and prepared for the operation. After meeting Robert Ellis, he required that he join them in their apartment for training. Saif's team of six was loyal followers of the jihadist philosophy. There were two men named Mohammed who went by Big Mo and Little Mo. These two were seasoned warriors who had killed hundreds of Syrian Kurds to ethnically cleanse the region. They took jobs in Manhattan in a Falafel restaurant right at Grand Central Station. The one known as Robert Ellis was an American Muslim who was trained in an Afghanistan terrorist training camp and reentered the United States to initiate a recruiting effort, but had to abandon the cause after being questioned by the local FBI. He worked at the Waldorf Astoria as a room service waiter. The final two, Shuja and Tamam, were good soldiers with very few exceptional qualities, which, per Aqeel, made them perfect candidates for the suicide assignment. They worked as taxi drivers for the Green Cab company. They shared a green Toyota Camry because they worked opposite shifts.

Ayman Zawahiri was twenty-six years old and easily persuaded to do whatever was asked of him. He was a true soldier who asked no questions but only did what he was told. His team consisted of his younger twin brothers, Aaqib, which means follower, and Darius, which means rich or kingly. The other three men, Eshan, Ghawth, and Rabah, were all recent graduates from the Afghanistan training camp for Al-Qaeda.

Ayman, Eshan, Ghawth, and Rabah were taxi drivers for the Yellow Cab Company in the Manhattan area of New York. The twins were waiters at the Palm Restaurant at 837 2nd Avenue, which was a quick taxi ride to Lenox and 113th Street, where the Mosque for the Islamic Brotherhood was located, and the place where information could be transmitted back to Iran. Since the mosque was just north of Central Park, it was also an excellent location for the taxi terrorists who needed to stay in touch. Their residence was the Stoneridge Apartments in Brooklyn, not more than a couple of miles from their counterparts with the same computer setup in their living room. They knew what was expected of them, and they were willing to die for their cause. They also believed it gave them special privileges to partake in the fruits of the flesh. It was something the group used to take their minds off what was to come on Eid al-Adha, the festival of sacrifice, which was to take place on the 12th of February.

The problem with being in one place for over twelve weeks is that somewhere along the way, a man might get into an attachment that he hadn't planned on. Ayman's brother Darius was just such a person. He had fallen in love with a dancer at the Payton's Gentleman's Club, which was located on the corner of 2nd Ave. and 39th street, right in the heart of Brooklyn. The girl went by the name Sophie, but her real name was Samantha Lockhart from Kansas. Darius couldn't get her out of his mind, and his twin and older brother were beginning to sense that they might have a major problem on their hands.

Darius met Sophie right after they arrived in New York and found himself spending a great deal of money on lap dances, just so he could talk with her. It wasn't long before the two began meeting after her shift at the club, where their relationship was consummated, and Sophie revealed her true identity to her new lover. She was warned by the other girls in the club to be careful, but Samantha was drunk in love with the stranger who had a thick Middle Eastern accent.

These feelings were giving Darius second thoughts about the suicide mission he had signed on for, and he planned on deserting his team and disappearing into the sunset with Samantha. He hadn't shared his plan with anyone but was compelled to tell his twin, who had always been his one confidant. Aaqib tried to convince his brother that this was a big mistake, but to no avail. Darius told his twin that he was going to take a small portion of the money that

Ayman was holding and simply be gone with Samantha. Aaqib pleaded with his twin to stop seeing the American girl. "She is evil, Darius. Nothing but bad can come from this union. Stop before you bring shame to our family." The twin begged. The dilemma for Aaqib was that his brother was dishonoring them all with this scheme, and as much as he loved his twin, he must report the situation to their older brother Ayman.

Despite all his bravado around people, Aqeel was terribly frightened for his life and wanted to stay out of Washington, D.C. He knew the safest place for him was Iran.

The American monster squad that had ruined his plot for the destruction of the subway system in England made it clear that they were after him. The only good thing about this threat was that it would help in his latest endeavor, because if they were after him, they couldn't spoil his latest attack. He had gone to great lengths to ensure that only a small group of select people even knew of the plan. Mansoor, his loyal soldier, was one of these special people. This was so very important for his overall goal to infiltrate the government. Once the Sears Tower was brought down, it would be the perfect opportunity for the young senator from Indiana to take center stage in uniting the country during the aftermath and thrusting himself into the national spotlight that could help him move closer to the White House. The only great concern about his hit team was the wild card known as Saif. Would he follow orders or do whatever he felt like at the time, which could hamper the success of the assignment? Aqeel could not concern himself any longer with such matters, for now he needed to catch a plane for home.

The terrorist soldiers were in New York for three months already and had another month before the attack would occur. They made friends at their jobs and gave no indication that they were anything but hard-working immigrants to America. The two leaders had already secured round-trip tickets. Zawahiri booked six round-trip tickets to Los Angeles on United flight number 443 departing at 8:30 am and arriving at 11:59 am. Al-Adel booked two tickets and three tickets at separate times for the Delta flight number 8788 for Phoenix departing at 7:20 am and arriving at 11:12 am. Each member of the team had carry-on luggage that fit neatly under the seat. They were designed with four fifteen-inch steel pokers threaded into the lining of the bags to look like part of the frame on x-ray inspection, but easily removed with a Velcro-covered trim. They were more than enough to subdue any passengers and a big enough threat to get the cockpit door keys from the lead attendant. Each night, both teams would go over all the possible scenarios that they might encounter and test each other as to the best solution for each. They were becoming well-orchestrated units all acting as one with one holy purpose...to kill infidels and destroy the fabric of America.

***

Michael began to formulate a game plan regarding New York. His goal was to find the two groups of extremists who were planning to kill more innocents in the name of their god. He decided to drive from D. C. and bring along all the weapons he might need to get the job done. The government was changing air travel and had established the Transportation Security Administration (TSA) under Homeland Security, and Michael knew that nothing he needed would get through their watchful eye. So, the tools of his trade were necessary. He thought to himself, Under no circumstances would these animals ever get on a plane.

With the limited amount of time left to them, he wanted to take Tess out to some special place and pop the question to her. Michael began making a few calls for a fancy restaurant. He decided to pick a place outside Washington, D.C., proper, and one that would be too expensive for the average FBI or CIA agent. He picked Restaurant Eve in Alexandria, Virginia, and called in a reservation for eight o'clock. Next, he called Tess on her cell. It was brief and basically a list of items he might need for the trip north. She let him know about her promotion, and all he could say was "it's about time." He hung up abruptly; then, he cursed his insensitivity and called her back.

"Sorry about that. I guess I was jumping into an operations mode, and I didn't want to do that today. Stop by your place and pick out something nice to wear. I'd like to take you out for a special evening together, someplace where I'm not likely to be so easily recognized." He said apologetically.

"I kinda got the feeling you were going in that Machine mode direction, but at least you're not blacking out anymore. How fancy a place is this?" she asked.

"I'll be wearing a new suit." He answered.

"Got it! I'll see you around seven?" she said in the form of a question.

"I'll pick you up at your place. Seven's great."

He got into his rental car and drove to Union Station, picked up a dark blue pin-striped suit with a white shirt and Bright blue silk tie. He stayed there an hour to have the alterations done and slipped the seamstress a hundred-dollar bill extra for her effort. From there, he drove to Nova Firearms and picked up two boxes of Fiocchi 9 mm shells and two boxes of Cor-Bon 380 ACP shells. He picked up some extra magazines and two lock boxes for each weapon.

His game plan was straightforward, and that was to go into the city, find the bad guys, and kill them before they could hurt anybody. His problem would be to kill twelve men so close together who most assuredly worked different shifts at different jobs, avoid contact with local police, and get out of town without increasing suspicion in the direction of Michael Angelino, who was, for now, considered dead somewhere in the Philippines. He looked up to Heaven and said, “I’m going to need your help on this one.”

Michael had one more stop, unrelated to the war but something he and God had discussed. The man behind the counter held the ring up and inspected it with a jeweler’s loupe. He looked at Michael and said, “This is a one-point-five-carat diamond that deserves certification. It’s flawless.”

“Wrap it up,” Michael said as he pulled cash out of his wallet. “Give me the cash price.”

“Cash price will be eight thousand dollars, sir.” The clerk said, hoping to shock the customer.

“Fine, put it in a nice box.” He replied without batting an eye. Michael smiled at the thought of using the enemy’s money. It was the least they could do to make me give up my normal life.

Chapter Eleven: Goodbyes

Tess was putting on her lipstick when there was a knock at her door. She glanced over at her cell. It was six fifty-nine. She gasped when she opened her door and saw him standing there. He had lost so much weight that this was the first time she saw him in something that fit just right.

"God, Michael, you look like a movie star." She finally said.

She immediately fell into his arms and kissed him softly as he gently dipped her for effect. He looked down at her and said in his best Clark Gable impression, "You're pretty awesome yourself, sweetheart. Shall we go?" He brought her back upright, spun her once, and said, "Wow!"

They made their way through the last part of commuter traffic, and Michael parked on a side street parking lot. They walked arm in arm down the cobblestoned street to the restaurant. It was a bit chilly in late January, but thankfully, there was no snow for a while, and Tess didn't bring a wrap. Michael removed his suit coat and draped it over her shoulders. Stars appeared as the sun descended into the horizon, and the street lights gave off the perfect lighting for a romantic evening. Once inside, Tess was taken by the cream-colored walls and the very decorative upholstery, all done in rich cinnamon and rust. There was an antique marble top oak credenza in the middle of the dining room with beautiful crystal glasses lining the bottom shelf. It was something any woman would appreciate. The chairs were lush with very high backs to provide some seclusion for the guests. Tess gave Michael his coat back as the dining room was nice and warm. The couple was escorted to a small table in the corner of the room. Michael removed his coat and set it on the chair next to her, just in case she got cold.

Within a moment, a tuxedoed waiter came to get a drink order. Michael chose a Duck Walk Vineyard Merlot 2000 from the extensive wine list, and the waiter bowed politely and was gone. The two talked about her day and the overall feeling in the Pentagon. Michael congratulated her again on her promotion.

"Most people were shocked about Mr. Avery, but Ted was almost business as usual. I thought that was sort of odd, since Chet hand-picked Ted for your old position. I guess I thought there was more of a relationship between them." Tess said, almost wondering out loud.

"He's moving up the food chain, and that doesn't give him a lot of time to mourn the dead," Michael said softly, giving her his two cents.

"He said he was convinced you were the one out there doing all the damage to the enemy, but then he says he believes you were killed while overseas. In his next breath, he told me that when you contact me, I'm to provide you with whatever information you need. Ted said our office will deny any involvement with you if you are caught or killed. He kinda sounds conflicted." She gave him a disbelieving look and a smile over what she had just told him.

"I'm more inclined to believe that he's hedging his bet in case I somehow survived the last battle and setting you up to get me caught just in case," Michael told her.

He looked deep into her eyes. "I don't want to talk shop, I would much rather tell you how very beautiful you are and how much I want to make love to you tonight." Tess blushed. The waiter arrived with the wine and menus. Michael turned to Tess and asked, "What is your pleasure, my lady?" "I'll have the Veal Oscar and the house salad." She told the waiter. Michael told the waiter, "Make that two."

The meal was perfect, and they held hands at the table as they shared intimate feelings for one another. After their plates were removed, Michael ordered a slice of New York cheesecake with raspberry sauce and two forks for dessert. After it arrived, he nervously told her, "Let's hold off on dessert right now, there's something I have to ask you."

"Okay." She responded with a curious look.

"You've known me a very long time, and you also know I have a pretty tight relationship with God. Well, He and I had a kind of talk the other day, and we decided that you and I should be married."

Before she could even respond, Michael pulled the ring box out of his pocket, got on one knee near her chair, opened the box, and asked her, "Will you marry me, Tess?"

The diners close by were eavesdropping and all held their breath waiting for the answer. The diamond caught the light just right, sparkling all over. Michael waited as Tess could not hold back the tears.

She asked him, "Are you sure about this?"

"Well, we either get married, or we have to go back to just being friends. If you know what I mean," he said with a devilish look in his eyes.

Tess got the message and said quickly, "Yes, absolutely yes."

The nearby audience applauded her response and politely went back to minding their own business. Michael put the ring on her finger and got back into his chair, still holding her hand. When the waiter came over, Michael asked if they could have a container for the cheesecake.

Once outside the restaurant, Michael put his coat back over her shoulders, and they held hands as they walked slowly back to his car. Tess kept looking at her ring. Michael finally broke the silence.

"I want to marry you tomorrow, Tess, before I have to leave you again."

"Tomorrow?" she asked, shocked.

"Unless you have other plans." He smiled.

"No, I'm pretty sure that'll work for me." Tess smiled back and then looked down at their hands together.

Once in the car, Tess got very business-like and wanted to find out what Michael might need from her and her department at the Pentagon. Michael gave her the names of the two terrorist leaders and asked her to see if they had any information concerning their whereabouts, but to keep her people as far from their location as possible. She agreed, knowing full well that any sightings of Michael could be an end to his war and the death of countless thousands.

"Sorry to change the mood, but my mind is racing, and I know we're running out of time. If I'm to be your wife, my job is to keep you as safe as possible, and I guess that means I'll be having more conversations with God, requesting he sends you home to me."

"Just so you know, God's not much of a talker, but he's a great listener," Michael said, smiling at her.

They made their way back to Michael's hotel room for a final night together. Once inside, Michael began to unzip her dress and helped her step out of it. His fingers found her bra snaps and flicked them open. He removed her bra delicately, lifted her into his arms, and gently deposited her onto the bed. He stood close by and began to remove his clothes while she watched, her beautiful, deep blue eyes glistening. He didn't say a word as he lied naked next to her. His last chore was to remove her panties, which he did with his thumb and index finger and slowly let them slide across her long, beautiful legs, and then dropped them to the floor. It was so quiet that it made them both tremble with excitement. His lips were soft and wet against hers. His touch was tender and loving. Michael was not in a hurry, and he wanted to relish every second with her. Tess could feel the increased tenderness in the way he was touching her. It was as if he might never see her again. She could sense it in his every movement. His eyes looked like blue gray crystals from the moonlight that reflected through the window. Tess was getting emotional to the point of tears, and they quietly moved down her cheeks. Would this be the last time he would touch me? She thought to herself. Michael was quiet, his lips moving over her body, examining every inch of her. His touch was electric as it sent waves of satisfaction from deep within her being, her sensitivity magnified. He loved taking his time as they moved in perfect rhythm, knowingly bringing her to the point of no return. Slow and methodical was his motion as he stirred within her. The quietness was deafening as her mind reeled about her special tomorrow and all the horrible tomorrows that would pass if he didn't make it back to her. She began to sob as they made love, and his hand found her face, and he gently caressed her face as if to say It will be alright, my love, and she understood his touch and all its meaning. Afterwards, they lied together holding on to each other as if the other might fall away. These two lovers understood the war that was waging outside, and knew it was important to just cherish the minutes they had left.

***

The morning light made its way through the window, and they were still in a tight embrace. Michael looked down at her as a tear escaped his eye. "After the wedding, it's going to be impossible to leave you," he said.

She was staring up at his face, trying to memorize every bit of him. "I know," she said sadly back to him.

They stayed together for another hour just looking at each other, until Michael finally made a motion and Tess understood it was time to let go of him.

The lovers got dressed and headed for the courthouse to get a license and have a civil ceremony. He went by the name David Devlin, which meant she would be Mrs. Devlin. It wasn't what she hoped for, but under the circumstances, it would have to do.

When they got back to his hotel room, he took her hand and began talking with God. "Heavenly Father, we are joined together with your blessing on us. Watch over us and keep us safe through the days ahead. Watch over my love as she waits for my return and bring me safely home to her. We ask this through Our Lord Jesus Christ." They both said Amen.

They made love to consummate their vows of love to one another, then showered together, soaping each other as an excuse to keep touching. There were a few words that needed to be said, but as he went out the door of the hotel room, he looked at her and said, "I will be back for you." She kissed her fingers and then pointed them at him. He understood there could be no more touching for now, so he caught her kiss and was gone. Tess lied alone in the hotel room, crying. She looked up to Heaven and said, "Please keep him safe, Lord, please."

Chapter Twelve: Surveillance

His car moved down the road, and his thoughts moved from Tess to the limited information at his disposal. Focus, Michael, focus. He thought to himself. Mansoor gave him the names of the soldiers and the town where they were staying, Bay Ridge, New York. He was sure they had changed their names for the operation. His mind was working overtime on possible interactions with the enemy when his phone beeped, indicating he received a text message. It was from Tess. Michael looked down to see the names and photographs of the two terrorists. She wrote, The Pentagon has information that the New York City Police Department was keeping tabs on Muslim citizens in the Bay Ridge community after 9/11, and indications are that this is still ongoing. She finished her communiqué with watch yourself. Using his thumb, he typed out "thanks" and sent it back to her. That meant that the police could be a major factor in his upcoming conflict. He said to himself, "I've gone into battle with worse odds."

Once on the Jersey Turnpike, he settled in for the two or three-hour drive, depending on traffic. Michael asked God to watch over him and keep him safe for Tess. Always the strategist, he watched the road but was clarifying his mission, which was clear. Kill the enemy before they ever get to a plane.

His mind raced over what he had done already and what was to come. He prayed for his savior to forgive him of any sins he committed during the war, and for those that were about to happen. He thought about Joshua and Sandi in California. He pressed the name on his phone. Joshua answered after the second ring.

"This is David Devlin with Acme Plumbing, just calling to see if the job I did is working out for you," Michael spoke into the cell phone.

"Hi David, yes, everything is fine. I do have some more work for you. When will you be able to come back out to the house?" Joshua questioned his father.

"Got a big job out of town, but I promise I'll call you as soon as it's over," Michael explained cryptically.

"Perfect, Dave, thanks for touching base, talk with you soon." Joshua hung up the phone and turned to Sandi, who was standing close by.

"It was my Dad. He's going to war again, said he'll be in touch as soon as he can."

Sandi put her arms around Joshua and told him what a great father he had. Josh nodded in agreement.

"We'd better pray for him just in case," Sandi said.

***

For the rest of the trip, he began to determine what he needed to accomplish his primary objective and what he would need to gather information necessary to get him closer to Aqeel. Killing him was an absolute necessity, one that Michael was going to enjoy. He knew that he needed to eliminate the targets that posed the biggest threat, and they were hiding in plain sight somewhere in Brooklyn.

A few hours later, he could see Lady Liberty; her light shining as night approached. He thought about how much he loved his country and the principles on which it was founded. He thought about how things were getting all screwed up by special interest groups who felt that the minority should make everyone else change. It seems the farther we move away from 9/11, the more our country is becoming less united, and the ridiculous fear of hurting Muslim's feelings has gone way overboard. He remembered Lincoln saying that America would never be destroyed from the outside. "If we falter and lose our freedoms, it will be because we destroyed ourselves." Michael saw it happening and wondered if our country would allow Lincoln's prediction to come true. His car passed the welcome to Brooklyn sign, and he went into war mode.

He first located the Islamic Society of Bay Ridge on 5th Avenue. He drove by slowly but decided to let his beard grow in for a few days before going to visit. Next, he found a one-bedroom apartment at Flatbush Gardens. It was a refurbished old brick building, and the unit had hardwood floors, a modest couch, a flat screen television, and a huge black and white photograph of New York from a view looking down on the city. It was clean and centrally located in the Bay Ridge area. He paid the manager a deposit and two months' rent in advance.

Michael stayed around the apartment the first few days, allowing his beard and hair to come in. His photographic memory was still intact, and the faces of the two men were embedded in his brain. So, on the fourth day, Michael trimmed and manicured his beard and made his way to the Islamic Center. He introduced himself to the Imam as Ben Santana and said that he was a medical device salesman and had just changed companies from a distributor in New Jersey to one in New York. He told the Imam he had converted to the Muslim faith while attending college. They enjoyed a friendly conversation. The Imam's name was Nader Nadershahi, and he was very sincere. Michael was good at seeing through people. This man was very devout, and that made him someone he wanted to know better. As Michael prepared to leave, he bowed slightly and said, "As-salāmu ʿalaykum." The Imam responded with a smile, "May the Lord be with you also."

His next move was to begin checking out the Gentleman clubs in the area, sure that these men would be allowing themselves to play before going to their deaths. The only one near the Bay Ridge area was a block away from Coney Island on Surf Street called Foxy's. Michael began doing his own brand of ethnic profiling once inside the joint. He would be looking for dark-haired men who might speak with an accent. They would be slightly suspicious when meeting anyone new. They would probably travel with another from their group and would be able to spend money freely since their source would have given them plenty of funds for their one-way journey.

He began watching who was getting the lap dances. He caught a glimpse of a tall Middle Eastern man having what appeared to be an argument with one of the girls in a corner of the room. Michael moved closer but kept his attention on the dancer swirling around the pole on stage.

"I told you this is my job, Shuja. Anyway, you don't own me," the pretty girl shouted to be heard over the music.

"Why must you move so close to all these men?" Shuja asked in desperation.

"If you really cared about me, you would get me out of here and take care of me," she barked.

"You know I can't do that, Candy, Saif would kill me." He pleaded for her to understand.

Michael continued to watch the stage, sure that the information Shuja just provided would be enough to allow Michael to have a starting point in his surveillance. He was sure this was a member of one of the teams. He moved away from them and got lost in the crowd, but his eyes were glued on Shuja. This could also be the weak link in their little group, and Michael was very good at exploiting that type of person. His mind raced back to the dentist chair and the interrogation of Bijan that ended with death.

"Stay focused," he told himself. A moment later, Michael was approached by a cute little brunette who had a name tag that read Honey.

"You need a dance, Grandpa," she said as she gently rubbed his short, gray, sparsely haired head.

"Gee, Honey, you might give this old ticker of mine a heart attack," he said in an old man's voice.

This made her giggle. She whispered in his ear, "Yeah, but what a way to go." She moved on, probably afraid she might really kill him.

Michael moved closer to the stage and dropped a few five-dollar bills into the G-string of the dancer. He was just another old fart getting some cheap thrills before going home to his wife. Nobody really paid much attention to him, and he couldn't be more pleased.

About two hours later, Shuja and another man left the lounge. Michael waited a few minutes before leaving, but reached the parking lot before they had a chance to leave in their car. His timing was impeccable. He slowly walked over to his car, all the time keeping a watchful eye on which car they got into and a license number that he could give to Tess in hopes that it would provide a local address. New York plates LEM 475 Late model Ford Explorer, dark blue with a light blue metallic top, he thought to himself. He started his car a few minutes after they left and followed far behind for just a few miles, then they disappeared into the night. Tomorrow will come soon enough, he thought to himself. He made his way back to his apartment.

He dropped his keys on the kitchen counter, an old habit that used to drive his wife, Elle, crazy. His mind took him back to Gettysburg, his house, and the sound of the keys hitting the Formica near the sink brought the memory of Elle's voice back to him.

"We have a perfectly placed key rack on the wall just where you wanted it, and oh look, the keys are on the counter again. God, Michael, I'm sounding like a nag."

Michael replaced the keys where they belonged, then picked Elle up off the ground and spun her around, laughing.

"I want to be mad at you, Michael, but you make it impossible," Elle said, giggling.

The past disappeared, and Michael picked up the keys, took them into his bedroom, and placed them on the dresser. He took out his phone and called Tess. It was after 2 AM, but Michael wanted to hear her voice badly, especially after watching those young bodies gyrating on the stage.

"Good morning," Tess said, half asleep.

"I know it's late, but I need you to get me some information first thing in the morning."

"Are you already on to them?" Tess inquired, already much more awake.

“I think so, New York plates LEM475 dark blue Ford Explorer, the sooner the better, Babe.” He cooed into the phone.

“I'm on it. Expect a call in the morning...oh, wait a minute, it is morning. I'll call you back at 7 am. I hope you're asleep when I call. Love you, Michael.” She said sweetly, then hung up. She grabbed a pen and quickly wrote what he said before she fell back to sleep and forgot.

Michael got into bed and started talking with God. Sometimes he just needed to work things out in his head, and he knew that God listened. “This threat to our country could be worse than 9/11, Lord, so guide me in the days ahead to find those who want to hurt America. Our country is going through a challenging time right now, and there are those who don’t believe in you and want to take you out of our schools and just about everywhere they can think of, but Lord, that is not most of us. I know we need to stand up for you, and I’m hoping that we Christians will stop turning the other cheek so much that we lose the freedom that you have provided us. “His fatigue was catching up to him. “You can tell by my bouncing around that I’m tired, I love you, Lord, and my future is in your hands. Amen.” He turned over to get more comfortable and was out cold.

Michael woke to the sound of his cell phone and grabbed it quickly before he lost the call. It was Tess. “The car is registered to Saif Mohammed. I’m guessing that’s Saif al-Adel. The address is 7225 6Th Ave. Brooklyn. How’d you sleep?”

“Good. I’ll talk to you later. I want to get started. Love you, Tess.” Michael said sincerely.

“I love you too. Please be careful. Bye.” She answered.

Michael pulled out his cell phone and punched in the address. A quick twenty-seven minutes by car. That could be a quick disposal of the terrorist garbage, but he needed the location of the other team. He knew he would be hitting the local Gentlemen's clubs in and around the area in hopes that he could locate the other team. So, he drove by the address and made a few passes to see how the streets intersected because with increased police presence in the area, it meant he needed to extricate himself without being seen upon completion of his mission. Everything so far was pointing to a nighttime operation, but it was a bit too soon to be sure. He stopped into a local Muslim store and purchased a prayer rug that was near the neighborhood of the mosque, and made his way there to feel out the Imam.

After Morning Prayer, he reintroduced himself and asked if the Imam had some time to talk. The religious nodded, and they made their way into his office. Michael was watching everything, even the way the man walked.

He scanned the room. It was an unpretentious space with a reproduction of the writings of the Koran framed on the wall behind a mahogany desk that showed the wear of many years of use. There was nothing that indicated funding from an outside source, but his conversation might bring something to light, and Michael would not let Soho happen again.

"What can I do for you, Ben?" The Imam asked as he directed Michael to a chair facing the desk. Michael waited till the cleric sat before beginning his tale of concern over what was happening to his country.

"Nader, first let me say that I love Allah, but I have many concerns over the escalation of hostility towards my country by our brothers of the faith. How do I bring others to our faith when all America hears is that we are a violent group of zealots?"

The Imam sat back in his chair. He considered Michael's eyes and said, "That is a very good question, Ben, and one that I have difficulty with, but we cannot allow the activity of the few to reflect the rest of us as a people of God. We must be examples of peace to those who know us and be kind to those we meet, knowing full well that their first impression of us will be foreboding and fearful."

Michael nodded, affirming what Nader said. Nader continued.

"What is happening today is as much political as it is religious. These terrorists do not want an American presence in their land and believe that to help America understand this, they must bring the horror of war to their land. Do I think this is the right course of action? Of course, it's not, but it isn't as black and white as the press might have you believe."

"I understand. Then the thing for me to do is be the best person I can be. Right?" Michael questioned.

"Not that complicated, is it?" Nader responded with a question, hoping it would give Ben some clarity.

"It's not. Thank you, Nader." Michael answered and began to get up.

"If I can be of any more help to you, Ben, please come back and see me." He said as he put out his hand. Michael decided to really test the water, "Do we have such zealots here, Nader?"

"Not to my knowledge, my friend."

The two men shook hands, and Nader said goodbye with "God be with you." Michael responded, "And also with you," and left the

Imam. Michael was confident that surveillance of Nader would not be necessary, and this would allow him to concentrate on his targets.

Michael went back to his studio, cleaned his weapons, ate something, and then took a nap. He woke a few hours later to the sound of his cell phone ringing. He missed the call, saw it was Tess, and redialed right away.

“What’s up, kid?” He asked in a way that made her tingle.

“I’ve got a bit more information that could prove beneficial regarding the terrorists. We got a photograph from near Times Square of Robert Ellis speaking to a Taxi driver who appears to be Ayman Zawahiri.”

“Ayman, I’ve got. Who is Ellis?” Michael asked.

“He’s been under surveillance for some time. He’s an ex-patriot who has embraced the Muslim extremist movement. I think he might be involved in some way. He works at the Waldorf Astoria. I’m sending you a close-up picture of him. I hope it helps.” She expressed concern for Michael’s welfare.

“I think I’m liking you in your new position. Keep looking out for me, sweetheart, and I might make it home.” Michael said with a chuckle.

“By the way, see if you can get intel on Aqeel Gabany’s whereabouts.

“I will. You'd better come home.” She snapped back.

“Okay, I’m off for now. Love you, Tess.” He said as a matter of fact.

"Love you back." Tess hung up the phone with her hand remaining on the receiver. When he said he loved her, it just took her breath away.

Chapter Thirteen: Misperception

Ayman, distraught with emotion, screamed at his younger brother, "You are on a holy mission chosen by Allah, and you want to throw that privilege away by bedding an American whore. You have dishonored our family, Darius. Our law is clear: you must be killed."

Never thinking that his twin would reveal his confidence, the young love-struck soldier pleaded that Aaqib had misunderstood their conversation. "I only told her I would leave with her, but I never would. I told Aaqib what I told her. It wasn't real. My duty is to Allah.

The thought of killing his brother was sickening to him, and he wanted to find any excuse to avoid his family duty. The misunderstanding story sounded plausible. "I will speak with our brother, perhaps it is as you have said, only an error. He put his arm around his young brother's neck and squeezed tightly with affection. "It's like you to lie for pussy."

Ayman left the room knowing that he must do something to correct this problem. He called his other twin on his cell phone. "Aaqib, what is the name of the whore our brother is seeing?"

"She goes by the name Sophie." The twin answered quickly.

"Keep your brother busy tonight on the computer, tell him I want him to put in extra hours on the simulator, tell him I have decided he will be our pilot after the takeover of the plane," Ayman instructed.

***

Robert Ellis was a lost soul who was searching for a cause that would make him important. He grew up in the New Jersey public school system, where socialist teachers indoctrinated him into believing that most of the terrible things that were happening around the world had their origins in the United States, and that our government was trying to control the lives of not only its citizens but everyone, everywhere. What better way to rectify this situation than to align himself with a group bold enough to do something about it?

In his second year of college, he was introduced to the Muslim faith by some radical students who were demanding that the United States leave the Middle East. Finally, the young distorted mind found something to hold on to, something to believe in. Yes, something that verified all the information he had assimilated through the school system. He made his way to Afghanistan, where he found his way to a terrorist training center. He excelled in the program, and his native language could be used as a major asset to the cause. Upon completion, he was sent back to the United States to bring others into the fold.

When 9/11 happened, he stood in his New York apartment living room shaking with excitement that the Muslim's version of Lexington and Concord had begun their war with the imperialists. Within weeks of the towers going down, Robert was brought in by the local FBI regarding his anti-American activity. Robert denounced the Muslim attack on 9/11 and claimed to the authorities that he returned to New York to restart his life. The FBI thought the young man was very intelligent and articulate, and took him off their suspect list of possible radicals in the city. Not long after this, he was contacted by Aqeel Gabany to participate in the plot to bring down one of the largest buildings in the United States and become the American representation of Al Qaeda. He would finally be a somebody.

Robert was a sadistic monster whom everyone in the two jihadist teams knew had issues with women. He was raised by two Aunts who nagged him incessantly until he beat one, causing her to be hospitalized just before his sixteenth birthday. This got the troubled youth put into a boy's prison until he turned eighteen years of age. His dysfunctional personality prevented him from ever having a female relationship, and although never mentioned by the group, the consensus was that he might have an interest in men.

Robert had just finished his shift at the Waldorf and was making his way to The Ridge when Ayman pulled his cab near to the curb. Robert got in without hesitation and asked why he was being contacted. Ayman explained the inconvenient situation his team was encountering and asked him to eliminate his younger brother's distraction. The American traitor knew the Gentlemen's club his alternate team frequented and went there that very night.

It was a very busy Saturday, and the bouncers had their hands full with a large group of sailors who had just gotten shore leave after six months at sea. Security didn't have their eyes on the girls all the time. For Robert, this meant he could do what he needed to do and never be seen. Knowing that he would not have to deal with Darius, he quickly found Sophie and asked for a lap dance.

The young woman knew her craft well and began to gyrate just over his pelvic region, only allowing her lower region to contact his groin occasionally, as she moved with the music. When she finished, Robert showed her two hundred-dollar bills and then placed them into her sequined bra. For Sophie, this meant paying attention to this guy because she could go home with a lot of money. After sharing the traditional watered-down cocktail with her guest, she asked if he would like a more private dance. He nodded with enthusiasm, and the couple went hand in hand into a darkened room near the back of the club. The customary nod by a bouncer to enter the back area was missed because a fight broke out as two sailors argued over who would get the next lap dance by a very beautiful blonde exotic dancer, and the back-room bouncer lost sight of his position for a few minutes.

Robert sat tensely as the young woman moved her body over his. The back room allowed for much more contact with very little restriction, and at the girl's discretion, it could mean a happy ending for the customer. Sophie wanted as much money as her client had in his pockets, so she gave him all. First, she sat on his lap facing him, then lifted herself ever so slightly, and she moved her pelvis rhythmically over his semi-erect member. Once she was sure she had gotten his full attention and made him physically ready, she turned with her back to him but continued to attack his crotch with the intention of bringing her customer to a climax. Robert's left hand slowly moved up to her neck, barely brushing up against her soft skin. She instinctively moved her head back, arching her back slightly to let him smell her hair as she moved seductively over his groin. His right hand holding his switch blade knife moved quickly to her throat and sliced her from the left side of her neck to the right. His left hand covered her mouth in the same instant. It was done. He lowered her to the floor and made his way out the back-emergency exit, which alarmed the minute he activated the metal bar downward. He ran through the alley past an old man walking slowly with a cane, who almost knocked him over, and a moment later was lost in the crowd of weekend traffic. The old man was The Machine, and his photographic memory recognized the runner as Robert Ellis.

Pandemonium ensued after Sophie's body was found, and within minutes, police arrived to ensure the crime scene was unaltered. The girls were screaming at the dead body of their friend. Bouncers stood in front of all the exits. Patrons were being crowded into one room, and the police were waiting for the arrival of the lead detective assigned to the case.

Detective Roger Jaeger was a seasoned officer who had been on the job for almost twenty years. Over six feet tall and just slightly graying at the temples gave him a fatherly look. Roger had a reputation for being a hard-nosed cop; some of his peers thought he was too rough, but he had a knack for closing cases. His partner, Thomas Knipe, on the other hand, was a soft-spoken man who did everything by the book and had developed a tolerance for Jaeger's abrasive personality. The two men arrived.

There was a lot of yelling and confusion with people wanting to leave and many who were drunk and disorderly, while others were being verbally abusive to the cops who had controlled the scene. Jaeger could see that order was needed quickly.

"When can we get the fuck out of here?" one of the sailors in the crowd yelled out as Jaeger walked past.

The detective stopped in his tracks and grabbed the man by his uniform. "Arrest this jerk for obstruction." A policeman standing by handcuffed the man and read him his Miranda Rights.

The room got very quiet after that. The next four hours were spent interviewing customers and staff to ascertain what and who might have had reason to murder this woman. The girls of the club were sobbing during their interview, but provided the detectives with information about Sophie's real name, Samantha Lockhart, and that she had a boyfriend. The girls told Roger and Thomas that she was upset because Darius called her to say he couldn't make it tonight, which meant that she had to tolerate being groped by the hands of customers. The lead detective threw more questions at the girls, hoping to get a bit more information about the boyfriend, who would either have a look of shock at the news of his girlfriend's death, or the phony overproduction of emotion that detectives found to be a telltale sign of guilt or at least some form of involvement. Roger was a bit surprised that none of the women knew where the boyfriend lived or had his telephone number. He made one of the girls take him into the changing room to find Samantha's cell phone and other personal belongings. He took the phone from her dressing table and scanned her recent calls first. Darius showed up three times. Roger pressed the call button and waited for an answer.

"Samantha, what's wrong?" the voice asked.

"This is Detective Roger Jaeger. Is this Darius?"

"Yes, why do you have Samantha's phone? What has happened?"

Jaeger paused for only a moment but answered with the sad news. He followed with a request to interview Darius, who was suddenly unresponsive after being told that his girlfriend was dead.

"Yes, I will come to the club right now." Darius finally answered.

"Thank you very much." The detective concluded and hung up.

The officer's sixth sense told him that this man could not have been involved, but might enlighten him as to who would want to hurt her. Roger thought of the alternative, which would be a maniac who wanted to hurt women, and that was something completely different, and would mean more bodies would be showing up. His experience told him it was an old boyfriend or a patron who was rejected by her. Roger made his way back to the main room, where he measured the faces of everyone, hoping for a tell, something that would denote guilt or remorse or knowledge of what happened. He was disappointed with the scan, but watched as his partner, Tom, was systematically interviewing each person. Jaeger took a seat at the bar, asked the bartender for a Diet Coke, and waited for the boyfriend.

Not too very far away, Darius already had a feeling as to who did this. He called Ayman, who was in his cab with a fare. He asked his brother if he knew what had happened.

"What are you talking about?" he lied.

"Samantha is dead," Darius answered into the phone.

"What happened, my brother?" Ayman questioned.

"I'm on my way to the club to find out, but I thought you should know," Darius said, hoping for a confession.

"You don't think I had anything to do with this horrible thing," Ayman questioned with horror at what his brother might be thinking.

"Where is Aaqib?" he asked his brother, trying to eliminate the obvious suspects.

"He's at work, Darius. How could you think such things?" Ayman challenged his brother's suspicions.

"I'm on my way to the club to speak to detectives," Darius said, changing the subject.

"Be very careful what you say, brother. Do not give the police any cause to investigate you or us," the older brother cautioned.

"I understand, Ayman." He said, then hung up.

***

Michael was close to the entrance of the gentleman's club when he saw police cars arrive, surrounding the building. He moved across the street and joined many pedestrians who had gathered to see what had happened. Michael was a true believer that there was no such thing as a coincidence. Police all around the club and Robert Ellis running from an emergency exit just made him feel there might be a connection.

It didn't take long to get the information that a young dancer was murdered. He stood and watched as a young Middle Eastern man made his way toward the entrance. He heard him say that he was called by Detective Jaeger to come down. The police officer at the door let him in. As people were being released to go, Michael approached one of the girls who looked like she might work at the club, mostly by what she wasn't wearing.

"What happened in there?" Michael asked like a concerned patron.

"One of the girls had her throat slit." She responded, frustrated. "I gotta get into a better line of work."

Michael was putting the pieces together quickly. Robert Ellis was a part of the suicide squad, and one of the guys in their group must have gotten too close to the girl. He surmised that she had to be eliminated. Michael decided to wait around and follow the young man who went in. If he were a part of the killer group, he might be able to be turned.

Sometime later, Darius came out of the club after seeing his girlfriend dead on the floor of the private booth area and being questioned by the detective. He was distraught. He noticed an old man who appeared frail in clothes that looked like he must have been a larger man at one time, coming up to him. The man greeted him with As-salāmu ʿalaykum. The man returned the greeting "Alaykum as-salamu."

Michael asked, "Did you know her?"

"Yes, we were engaged to be married," came his response.

"Oh, I'm very sorry. My name is Ben."

Darius responded only with his name. "Darius."

"I work in the city for Aramark food service delivery." Michael lied thinking of the biggest company he knew in New York. He wanted to establish a relationship with Darius.

"My brother and I work at the Palms as waiters. I think your company delivers to our restaurant." He said, seeing that they had some type of connection.

They began to walk away together just as Jaeger and Knipe came out of the club.

"Who's that guy with Darius?" Jaeger questioned his partner as he scratched his unshaved face.

"He looks very wanted poster familiar to me."

Thomas answered, "I've definitely seen him before."

The detectives finished interviewing the employees and patrons and made their way back to the precinct. Detective Jaeger sat at his disorganized desk and rummaged through a pile of faxed FBI person of interest posters until he stopped at the face he thought was outside the strip club. The problem was that the more he looked at the older, heavy-set man in the picture, the less it looked like the person he saw with the grieving young man a few hours before. He threw the poster across his desk over to Detective Knipe and asked, "Is this the guy we saw last night?"

Tom looked carefully at the poster but could not verify that it was the same person. "It kinda looks like the guy, but I sure wouldn't bet on it." The face on the poster was much heavier with a well-manicured beard.

"The guy last night looked about ten years younger and fifty pounds thinner and had a bald head. He looked more like a religious cleric than in this picture. I don't think it's the same guy. Anyway, it says here this guy was last seen in the Philippines." Tom told his partner.

"I think we need to visit that young man again." Jaeger decreed.

"You want me to call him?" Thomas chimed back the question as he got up to get his third cup of coffee.

"Yeah, give the kid a call," Roger responded with a yell to Knipe, who was almost at the coffee pot.

***

Ayman and Aaqid stood over their brother, consoling him over his loss. The older one blamed the sick, perverted country they were ready to attack. The twin just put both hands on Darius and massaged his shoulders as he wept uncontrollably. The cell phone on the table rang, and Ayman picked it up.

"Hello," he said into the phone.

Knipe informed the person who he was and asked to speak to Darius.

"I am his older brother. He is very upset right now. Can I have him call you later?" Ayman asked politely.

"It's important we speak to him tomorrow. Can he come down to the seventy-third precinct on New York Avenue?" the detective inquired.

"I'll tell him. He will be there after morning prayer, okay?" Ayman asked.

"That will be fine," Knipe answered and hung up the phone.

He turned to Jaeger and said, "We don't want to profile this guy, but something is rotten in Denmark." Jaeger nodded as he stuffed a coffee-soaked, stale donut into his mouth.

***

Michael got to his apartment and sat at his kitchen table. He was sure that the distraught young man was a part of the suicide squad he was after, but didn't want to tip his hand until he had done some more surveillance. He had now found both teams and began to formulate a plan for their disposal. He prayed silently for guidance from God; then he began writing out what he knew, and his scheme became clear. He would pit them against each other, allow them to do most of his work, and then go in and finish the job with a flair for the gruesome.

Chapter Fourteen: Setting the Table

The following morning, bright and early, Michael arrived at the mosque for morning prayer. The Imam approached Ben before prayer started. They shared a greeting and spoke about the discussion from the previous day. It was just enough time for Darius to notice the two together, and that is what Michael wanted: to give the young man an inkling that he could be trusted. They joined each other after prayer, and Michael asked him how he was doing.

"I'm doing better today. The police asked several questions about my relationship with Samantha and if I knew of anyone who would want to hurt her. I told them I didn't, but they called and asked me to come down to speak with them again sometime this morning." Darius shared with his new friend.

"Do you think they suspect me?" he asked

"The police are probably just being thorough," Michael assured him.

"I saw something last night when I was on my nightly walk. I don't know if it's important, but as I passed the club, I noticed a dark-haired, thin man coming out of the back door of the club. Normally, I wouldn't have given it a second thought, but the young man looked a bit crazed, and he almost ran me over as he headed down the alley. I thought he had a knife in his hand, but my eyes aren't what they used to be, so I can't be sure."

"Would you recognize him if you saw him again?" Darius asked with anticipation.

“I could do better than that, I could draw him, I used to be quite a good artist when I was a younger man,” Michael told the heartbroken young man.

“Let’s go into the Nablus Sweet Shop for coffee,” Darius suggested.

Once inside, a beautiful woman with her head covered approached the table and greeted them in the Muslim language. Darius asked for two cups of coffee and sweet rolls and waved her away. Michael took the paper placemat and turned it over, took a pen from his pocket, and began drawing a face. At first, it didn’t look like anyone the terrorist knew, but slowly Michael began adding details until he finished by adding a pencil-thin moustache. Darius’s face winced, which let Michael know he recognized the image on the paper.

“I’m sorry, I used to be a better artist, but now my hands don’t work so well.”

“No, no, you have done an outstanding job. May I have it?” Darius asked with excitement.

“Of course, perhaps it can help the police find him,” Michael suggested.

“Yes, I will be sure to give it to them this morning. Thank you so much, Ben,” he answered just as the coffee and sweet cakes arrived.

Michael had set the wheels in motion and was curious as to how Darius would handle this important bit of information.

***

Ted Hobson relished the idea that in a very short time, he moved up the ranks to a position of great authority. He was a man who was used to getting what he wanted, and now that he had the position, he wanted the girl to go with it. Ted was a good-looking man, with deep brown eyes and hair, a strong chin, and a physique that indicated he worked out regularly. He had his eye on Tess Lamia the minute they met, and now that Michael Angelino was presumed dead and out of the picture, he was going to make his move.

Tess arrived and went directly to her office. She sat down and looked at her left hand to admire her rings. She didn't notice her boss's arrival.

He looked at her hand in disbelief. "Is there something you want to tell me?"

"Oh yes." She waved her hand nonchalantly. "I got married yesterday. His name is David Devlin, and he's a salesman for a medical device company out of Philadelphia." She lied very convincingly.

"Well, when did you meet him?" Ted asked.

"We've known each other for years, but he has always been just a friend. He came into town last week and asked me out and literally swept me off my feet, and well, we just did it." She said her eyes sparkling as she thought about the man she loved.

"Well, I guess congratulations are in order." Ted sighed like the wind was out of his sails.

"Thanks, Ted."

"So, when can I meet him?" he asked curiously.

"The next time he's in town, I'll have you over for dinner, okay?" she lied sweetly.

"Okay then. I only came in to discuss information that just crossed my desk about chatter we're getting from our intelligence that something is coming up on the next Muslim holiday called Eid al-Adha, the festival of sacrifice. I believe it is on the 12th of February. What do our analysts suggest is a possible target?" Ted inquired firmly.

"Well, our top people are suggesting another plane attack, but can't give us a specific target because the internet chatter only states that an attack is coming. The terrorists are quickly adapting to our technology and altering the way they communicate." Tess explained.

"We'd better come up with something soon, or we're going to have another 9/11 to deal with, and the fallout from that might be our jobs," he said just before he left her office, still reeling at the announcement of Tess's marriage.

***

Darius arrived at the seventy-third precinct and was escorted to Jaeger's desk. The old veteran detective wanted to make the young man feel at ease, so he was acting contrary to his gruff demeanor. "How are you doing today?"

The nervous suspect replied, "I don't have any answers as to why anyone would want to kill Samantha."

"We saw you with someone last night. Who is he? Roger asked directly.

His name is Ben. I don't know his last name. He is from our Mosque. He wanted to be sure I was alright last night." Darius replied.

"How long have you known him?" Roger continued to question.

"We met last night and had breakfast this morning." Darius answered and then asked, "Why are you asking me about this old man?"

"We thought he might have said something to you about the case. Right now, we're looking for any leads, and he just looks familiar to us. It's probably nothing. Do you know where he lives?" Jaeger persisted.

"You should probably ask our Imam because Ben and he spend time together, but what does he have to do with the death of Samantha?" Darius asked, agitated.

"Okay. Okay. You're probably right. Do you know who her last boyfriend was? Any chance this guy wasn't happy about her seeing someone else?" Roger asked, changing the subject.

"She never told me about anyone else, and I never saw her even get into an argument with any of the customers at the club. She was how do you say it? An awesome girl." After Darius said this, he became emotional again, his eyes tearing.

Jaeger knew this guy wasn't involved, but something was making the hairs on the back of his neck stand straight up, and that made him nervous. So, he continued to pry out as much information as he could.

"How long have you been here in America?"

"About three months."

"What brought you to our fair country?" He asked.

"Why are you asking me this kind of question, because of the color of my skin? Shouldn't you be looking for whoever did this horrible thing instead of harassing me?"

Jaeger wanted to see how far he could take the young man, but he didn't want a lawyer showing up screaming racial profiling. He could see that Darius was on the edge, so he let it go.

"Sorry, Darius, but this murder investigation is going slowly, and that bothers us. Tell you what, if we uncover anything, we'll keep you in the loop. Okay?"

Darius calmed down, thanked the detective, and left the office. He walked slowly down the street, pulled the drawing from his pocket, and thought about how he would handle what he knew came from his older brother. He briefly thought about Ben and decided he would tell him about the police questions. His anger grew with each step closer to the apartment. Images of his twin conspiring with Ayman to eliminate the threat to their mission flashed before his eyes. Tears were streaming down his face as he thought of his beautiful Samantha and their love that was now lost forever. He was going to kill Robert Ellis before their mission, this he promised himself, and he would deal with his older brother as he went from depression to anger. Darius had his own agenda, and it would take precedent over their jihad. By the time he got to the door of his apartment, he was composed and complacent.

Ayman called him from his taxi in Manhattan to find out what the police said to him. "Darius, how did it go at the police station?"

"Fine, they have an eyewitness who saw a man running from the emergency exit with a bloody knife in his hand." He lied into his cell phone.

There was a moment of silence that confirmed Darius's suspicions. Then Ayman said, "That's great, perhaps the monster will be caught."

"Yes, catching the monster is all I can think about," the younger brother replied and hung up.

***

Michael returned in the evening to the Islamic Center for evening prayer and to spend some more time with the Imam, in the hope that Nader might be able to give some insight into the minds of these extremists. Since he was in the middle of a war with them, knowing how they think could become an asset, and he wanted to challenge the cleric to be sure he wouldn't become a target.

"It's good to see you again, Ben," Nader said with enthusiasm.

"Nader, can we talk a bit about what is happening with our brothers who have become killers of the innocent?" Ben asked sincerely.

"Of course, Ben, let's go to my office." He answered with a welcoming hand gesture.

Once inside the Imam's office with the door closed for privacy, the Imam asked Ben what he would like to discuss.

"These men who speak of Allah and kill even our own brothers of faith, how can this be the will of Allah?" Ben inquired.

"These men have taken the Koran out of context. Mohammed spoke of God as the one true deity with no equal. Our people were persecuted in the early days of our history, and Mohammed speaks of killing the infidel as killing anyone who does not believe as we do and who prevents us from practicing our faith." Nader explained.

"This I understand," Ben commented.

"They hurt those of us who just wish to praise God. This is a terrible time for our people right now because if these radicals continue, Muslims will be persecuted by non-believers who have become afraid of all of us, and this will lead us into just what the Koran says about us killing the infidel." Nader explained.

"I see," Ben said. "But what should we do?"

"That is the question, Ben. If we don't speak out against the radical faction, we are perceived as a threat to Americans. If we do speak against the jihadists, we are considered by them to be not true believers of the faith, and that makes us a target for their form of justice. We must pray for wisdom and understanding and the will of Allah." Nader said, putting his hands together as in prayer.

Ben reached out and held the cleric's hands in his own and said, "You are a very good man, Nader. Thank you for sharing with me." Ben said and then got out of his chair to leave.

"Did this help you, Ben?" Nader asked sincerely.

"More than you know," Ben said and left the room.

Michael left the meeting with a deeper understanding of a faith that is caught in a web of misunderstanding. For all his life, Michael thought that Jews, Muslims, and Christians all believed in the same God, but this god of the Muslims was indifferent to his people. There was no real relationship with the Almighty, and yet they're told that they should read three holy books besides the Koran: the Torah (the first five books of the Bible), the Psalms, and the New Testament. They are said to believe that the Gospels are a true and accurate historical account of the life of Jesus, but that it is not inspired by God and that Jesus did not die on the cross, but was replaced by someone else, possibly Judas. The information would not change what The Machine must do, but it did help him understand his enemy.

***

Jaeger's men found a trail of blood drops outside the emergency exit at the back of the club, but they only lasted a block before they stopped. Whoever murdered the girl must be within walking distance of the club. Roger thought to himself. He typed out a list of known felons in the area. The computer quickly spit out a list of thirteen individuals.

"Ricco, you and Edwards check these guys and let me know if something isn't kosher," he said.

The next step would be to research persons of interest in the area. There were about forty-seven men and women on the list; most of them were foreign nationals, but the name Robert Ellis showed up, which seemed very strange to him, so he looked up his name for more specifics. What he found sparked his interest because Ellis had issues with women.

"Tommy, let's go. I got a hunch we may have found just the guy we're looking for." Roger barked to his partner.

"Okay, Rog," came the response as Tom finished his coffee.

Robert Ellis was at the hotel where he worked when The Machine found him. Michael was dressed in a business suit and dark glasses, checked in under the name Stan Santana, and was given a beautiful room on the twentieth floor. Prior to entering room 2016, The Machine put on his work gloves to ensure there would be no sign of him remaining after his departure.

The room was wallpapered with a peach color and accenting brown vertical stripes. The valance and curtains were also done in vertical stripes of green and brown, giving the room a larger appearance. The furniture was all dark cherrywood, which included a small desk, and hanging on the wall was a flat screen television. Michael picked up the hotel phone from the end table and called room service.

"I'd like a corned beef sandwich on rye bread with chips and a diet Dr. Pepper." He requested.

"And if he's quick about it, there'll be a big tip for him." Michael hung up the phone and pulled out his hunting knife. A big tip, he thought to himself as his finger contacted the tip of the blade.

He walked around the room to get completely acclimated, anticipating any struggle that might ensue. He thought long and hard about this kill, and it needed to be brutal. So, he waited, turning on the television for the local news.

"Room service." A voice called out with a knock at the door.

Michael opened the door and was pleased to see Robert Ellis with the tray of food. He asked that the platter be put on the desk. As the bellhop put the plates and soda down, he felt something being forced into his mouth. Michael had one hand on the washcloth and the other on his 9mm. The butt of the weapon struck the young man's head, rendering him unconscious.

Michael prepared the bed as if it were a dining room table, removing the bedspread, leaving the crisp white sheets, and placing the unconscious murderer upon it. He went into the closet and cut the cord from the iron using it to tie Robert Ellis's arms, then cut the rope for the drapes to tie down his feet. He went through his pockets and found a cell phone and keys. Michael wasn't sure how much time he had with his first victim of this battle, but he knew the police would be close.

Downstairs in the lobby, detectives Jaeger and Knipe were speaking with the hotel manager, asking to speak to Mr. Robert Ellis. The manager indicated that he was very busy, and they would have to wait until he returned. The two men sat in the lobby patiently.

Robert's eyes began to open with a sudden look of horror when he realized a hand towel was shoved into his mouth, his arms and legs were tied up, and the television volume was turned up. The Machine spoke very softly to his captive and explained that he needed a bit more information about his group of international terrorists.

"We don't have a lot of time to play, Robert, so please answer truthfully and quickly, and let's avoid the torture part of this," he said politely. He grabbed the end of the towel and slowly removed it. Ellis tried to call out, but the towel was reinserted quickly.

"That was a costly mistake, Robert." The hunting knife was thrust into his right quadricep muscle, which caused severe pain but avoided any major vessels. Robert screamed through the towel, emitting very little sound, his eyes tearing, and his head jerking violently from the pain.

"Shall we try again, Robert?" The Machine questioned.

"When do the others return to your apartment?"

Robert proceeded to detail their work schedules and the fact that Saif al-Adel didn't have a schedule at all. He whimpered like a little girl, pleading to be spared. Michael asked him who put him up to killing Samantha. He responded quickly, "Ayman."

The Machine, hearing that, proceeded to fillet the young man. Robert, gagged, was forced to watch as his insides were carefully removed. The blood began to soak through the sheets and form a puddle on the floor. Robert was about to lose consciousness, but heard the icy voice whisper. "Now, I'm going to send you to hell." With that, The Machine plunged the huge blade into the man's exposed heart.

Michael went over to the sink in the bathroom, washed his gloved hands and face of blood splatter, then toweled dry and put the small towel into his pocket. He picked up half of the sandwich and ate it, took the bottle of Dr. Pepper, and left the room. Replaced his dark glasses and made his way down the elevator. He entered the grand lobby with its huge mosaic floor and beautiful blue stained-glass windows, and then noticed the two detectives at the counter demanding that they produce Robert Ellis. They didn't see his killer move quietly through the double doors and nod to the doorman. Michael took out his cell phone and asked to speak to Detective Jaeger. He was patched through to the detective's cell, and Michael said. "Officer Jaeger, Robert Ellis is in 2016, but he won't have too much to tell you. He killed the girl, so you can close that case."

"Who is this?" Jaeger yelled into the phone, but the line was already dead.

First blood was just served in this new battleground, and The Machine set the table. Time would need to be watched carefully because this was going down. Michael knew all about timing, and his clock was ticking.

Chapter Fifteen: The Blood-letting

Michael would have to move very fast to stay ahead of the New York police detectives. He watched the door of Robert Ellis's apartment. A young man without a beard stepped out, jiggled the door to make sure it was locked, and disappeared into the parking garage. The Machine knew the face to be that of Saif al-Adel. Michael went to the door of the apartment and knocked. When no one answered, he took Robert's keys and found the one that worked. He took only a few steps inside when he heard keys and the door opened. Saif returned unexpectedly, and the two men faced each other. Their eyes locked for a long instant.

The young terrorist attacked Michael with a tackle to his midsection, which brought both men to the floor. Saif got up quickly and kicked Michael, but in his second kick, Michael grabbed his leg and elbowed the thigh muscle. He followed up with a palm thrust to Saif's nose as hard as he could, which sent the nasal cartilage into the terrorist's brain, killing him instantly. He fell like a sack of potatoes, and The Machine was glad for the military training which taught him the maneuver. He moved the body into a bedroom and waited in the dark room. According to Robert Ellis, the last four men would be arriving between six and eight, each about an hour apart.

This was what The Machine was trained for: hide until the target was in his line of fire. He knew what needed to be done. Whoever walked through the door would turn on the lights and move forward, tired and probably hungry. The 9-millimeter he secured from Mansoor with a silencer was just enough to stop them forever. So, he waited and watched the door for his next target.

Ellis was very accurate when he was tortured. It was something you couldn't convince a politician was true, but The Machine knew different. Torture brought him accurate results. The door opened, and the right hand moved to the light. Michael was in the hallway. His target dropped some papers on the table and turned to go to his bedroom. Two steps from the hall, the tired taxi driver's head exploded with very little sound except for the blood and brain matter that hit the ceiling. The body was moved just past him in the hall. This time, he left the light on so as not to look suspicious.

Another hour and the door opened again, a few minutes later, another jihadist lied dead on the hallway floor. Michael turned on the television to a cop show, moved back into position, and again he waited. The smell of blood began to become noticeable. The Machine recalled lying under dead bodies for hours to get to his target. It was the way of war: kill or be killed. The door rattled again, only this time there were two men who entered the apartment. Big Mo and Little Mo got off together and came in for a quick meal. The larger man mentioned Foxy's just as the 9-millimeter put a third hole in his head. There was no delay as the next bullet struck Little Mo in his right chest, pierced the lung, and brought the soldier down and short of breath. He lied dying as Michael now took the time to ransack the rooms, where he found a 38 special loaded and a cache of money. He inspected it briefly and summarized that it was close to a hundred thousand, mostly in large bills. He came back to the dying man by the door, placed the 38 in his hand, held the hand close to his head, and pulled the trigger. The scene now looked like a domestic dispute gone wild. The sound of the weapon going off would hardly be noticed with the television blaring. He opened the front door and looked around. Once sure that nobody was paying attention, he walked out and down the side of the building to where he had parked the car. It wasn't more than ten minutes later that a police car pulled up, and two patrol cops made their way up to the apartment of Robert Ellis. Michael watched until he saw the two detectives from the Samantha murder arrive. He knew they would be busy for some time trying to figure out just who shot whom.

He quickly made his way to the Stoneridge Apartments and sat in his car with a view of apartment K. He didn't have to wait long before three Middle Eastern men departed the room and got into a small Toyota Corolla. He gave them plenty of room as he followed them to the Sunset Park area on 2nd Street and a place called Peyton's Playpen, one of the last cobblestone street adult bars.

He was remembering his attack at the San Bernardino strip joint, where a young exotic dancer was shot. He would try to avoid that from happening again, but he was sure that this was where they would die. He paid the admission price and entered the semi-dark room. There was a bachelor party going on with fifteen young guys slipping dollar bills into the G-string of a beautiful red-headed dancer who was gyrating around a pole in the center of the stage. The room wasn't very big, so finding his targets took only a few minutes. He watched from near the back and waited until one of the three decided to relieve himself. As he made his way into the john, Michael pulled out Betty and got her ready for action. The Middle Eastern man didn't even look up to see who entered. His face took on disbelief as the sharp blade moved across the neck of the terrorist so quickly he could only gurgle once or twice before he slumped over and died. Michael carried him into one of the two stalls and sat him on the toilet. He took a mop out of a bucket near the supply room, mopped up most of the blood, and used the handle to lock the door from the inside. He knew most guys who go to a gentleman's club only use the urinals, so no one would pay much attention to the locked door.

The bachelor party was getting a bit rowdy, so the security guys really had their hands full. The two terrorists were each getting a lap dance when Michael interrupted.

"Excuse me, gentlemen, but your friend just stepped out of the emergency exit, vomiting profusely. Is there someone I can call, or would you like to check on him?" Michael spoke like one of the security team and winked at the girls.

"We will attend to him," the taller of the two said with a thick accent.

"Right this way," Michael said as he directed them to the exit. His 9-millimeter was already out as they entered the alley.

"Where is…" was all that escaped his lips as his brain exploded on his partner. The second shot hit the bad guy in the neck, exploding the carotid artery, and in seconds, he choked to death on his own blood. The weapon was put away, and Michael went back to his car to finish his evening's work.

Michael knew the last three he would deal with were brothers. A part of him wanted to give Darius some satisfaction for the murder of the woman he loved, but The Machine wasn't making any promises.

The Machine stood at the door of apartment K and knocked meekly. Darius answered the door.

"As-salāmuʿalaykum." Ben greeted his friend.

"Alaykum as-salamu," Darius responded. "Come in, please."

Once inside, Ben noticed Ayman and Aaqid in the small kitchen. He nodded as Darius introduced his friend from the mosque. The two men nodded back but were a bit suspicious of the stranger.

“May I fix you a coffee?” Darius asked politely.

“I really don’t have too much time. I only came by to see how you were doing and to find out if my drawing was of any help to the police?” Michael asked sincerely.

“Did you see something that night?” Aaqid asked.

“I did. I made a second drawing that I think is even better.” The Machine reached into his pocket, pulled out the 9-millimeter, and shot Aaqid right between the eyes, quickly turned the gun to Darius, and shot him in the right chest. Ayman went for a knife on the counter but was shot in the right arm and right shoulder.

Michael knelt over Darius, who was in shock at what had just happened, and said, “I promise I will kill your brother for what he did to you. He then put a bullet in his head.

Ayman would die very soon, but not until Michael got some information about Aqeel.

“I need some information about the one who sent you,” Michael asked in a very soft voice.

“I have no information to give, you bastard,” Ayman answered defiantly.

“We’ll see,” Michael announced as he inserted the silencer into the shoulder wound. He pulled the trigger three times and allowed the bullets to disintegrate his shoulder, only leaving skin to hold the arm in place.

“How about now, Ayman?” The Machine asked.

“Fuck you!” The response came quickly.

Michael put the gun to his genitals, “How about now?”

Ayman spit at him, and an instant later, his penis exploded. He screamed from the sheer pain, but only gave The Machine a look of indignation and disgust.

"Okay, if you have nothing to tell me, then I will do this for your brother, who you betrayed for your cause, a cause that has only brought death to your brothers and now you." Michael put the gun into his mouth and pointed the weapon towards his brain; he pulled the trigger two more times to ensure that his brains were destroyed, just like their plan.

***

"I need to speak to the detective in charge of the stripper murder," Michael demanded.

A few minutes later, a voice came on the line. "This is Detective Jaeger."

"I left you a mess at the Stoneridge apartment, K. They were all terrorists with a plan to hurt America, now they'll all rot in hell."

"Who are you?" Roger asked.

"Just call me a response to the war," Michael said and then ended the call.

Chapter Sixteen: Needed Intel

Tess was in the car when her cell phone rang. She had set the ringtone to identify Michael and be sure that she could answer it without pretending she was talking with Acme Air Conditioning Services. A small detail, but one that needed fixing, since no one gets that many calls from an air conditioning company.

"I'm in my car. I love you. When will you be back?" she rattled without a breath.

"Assignment complete. Not one of those Jihadists is getting on a plane for their Eid al-Adha festival of sacrifice holiday." Michael reported in military fashion.

It took him a moment for her voice to finally register in his head, and the softer side of the soldier found its way to the surface. "I love you too."

"There are a few loose ends, but I should be back in D.C. soon," Michael told his new wife.

"Is there anything I can help you with?" she asked sincerely.

"It's Aqeel, I know he's not the boss, but he is definitely one of the main decision makers, and that makes him my next target. His death will let it be known that this force opposing them is getting deeper into their ranks, and that will cause them to become more afraid. Fear works in my favor every time." Michael explained.

"I've already started an investigation of Aqeel Gabany. It began after Chet's death. He has been classified as a person of interest but is not on our no-fly list, which means, according to our people, he is either in or out of the country." Tess told him.

"I have his cell phone number. It's 202-555-0666, call me if it pings. I'll wait for your call before I leave New York. Love you." Michael hung up.

He didn't have to wait too long for results. His phone rang. Tess gave him the information he requested. "Aqeel is on the move, heading west towards Indiana's capital of Indianapolis."

"Why would he be going there?" He wondered out loud.

Michael couldn't make sense of this information. He thanked her and ended the call. He sat for some time thinking about the information he had acquired, but nothing to tie him to that city. He hated to do it, but he needed to use his informant.

***

Mansoor Amoli was recovering well from his knee injuries. He was able to get around using two canes and had adjusted to a life without a finger. It was a constant reminder of where his loyalties were to reside. His wife, Adiva, noticed a change in the way he treated her and their twin sons. She had felt the back of his hand on many occasions. The tyrant who used to constantly order them around like slaves had become kind and attentive towards her, and supportive of their sons. She was concerned that he was spending a great amount of time reading the Bible, but was thrilled with his change. Finally, she asked him why he was interested in the book invalidated by some Muslims. He brought her into his office and shut the door behind her. He asked her politely to sit. He took the small Bible from his drawer and opened it to the New Testament, the gospel of John, and read out loud, but only so she could hear it.

In the beginning was the Word, and the Word was with God, and the Word was God. He was with God in the beginning. Through him all things were made; without him nothing was made that has been made. In him was life, and that life was the light of all mankind. The light shines in the darkness, and the darkness has not overcome it.

"The book is speaking of Jesus, my love." Mansoor turned a few more pages and read again.

When Jesus spoke again to the people, he said, "I am the light of the world. Whoever follows me will never walk in darkness but will have the light of life." The Pharisees challenged him, "Here you are, appearing as your own witness; your testimony is not valid." Jesus answered, "Even if I testify on my own behalf, my testimony is valid, for I know where I came from and where I am going. But you have no idea where I come from or where I am going.

"What does it mean, Mansoor?" his wife asked softly.

"We have been taught that Jesus was a great prophet, but that he was not the Messiah spoken about in the Old Testament, but his own disciple has written that Jesus is the one and only son of God.

Jesus calls himself the light of the world. Our faith has taught us that Jesus did not die on the cross, but it is documented in historical documents, not just the Christian Bible, that a man named Jesus was put to death by the Romans and that eyewitnesses said he rose from the dead. Josephus, a historian at the time, wrote about this Jesus, whom he called the anointed one, and wrote how he did many incredible things and was seen alive again after his death. Mansoor quickly turned a few more pages to John 20:24-29.

He began to read to her again.

Now Thomas, one of the Twelve, was not with the disciples when Jesus came. So, the other disciples told him, "We have seen the Lord!" But he said to them, "Unless I see the nail marks in his hands and put my finger where the nails were, and put my hand into his side, I will not believe."

A week later, his disciples were in the house again, and Thomas was with them. Though the doors were locked, Jesus came and stood among them and said, "Peace be with you!"27 Then he said to Thomas, "Put your finger here; see my hands. Reach out your hand and put it into my side. Stop doubting and believe." Thomas said to him, "My Lord and my God!" Then Jesus told him, "Because you have seen me, you have believed; blessed are those who have not seen and yet have believed."

"My darling Adiva, I am telling you that the same Jesus who our faith speaks of is not a good prophet, but the son of God and is God, but he is not a God who is far above us, uninterested and aloft. He is a God who loves us more, my darling, than I love you. This God wants us to be with him forever. He quickly turned back to John 14:6 and read to her as she stared at him in amazement.

Jesus answered, "I am the way and the truth and the life. No one comes to the Father except through me.

Upon reading the verse, Mansoor fell on his knees in front of his wife and apologized to her for the way he had treated her through their years together. He was sobbing openly at her feet. Adiva was overwhelmed with emotion. Who was this man professing love to her? This man she had given her love to so many years before. He was a man she trusted completely and loved completely, and although she was a bit confused by all he told her, she believed him as he looked up at her with tears streaming down his face. She kissed him and used her thumbs to wipe his emotion from his face. The two had never felt closer to one another, and they remained in a warm embrace until his cell phone rang.

"Mansoor, I am in need of some intelligence." The cold voice demanded.

"Adiva, I need to take this call." He told his wife gently.

Once she left the room, he asked his boss what he needed. Michael could tell that Mansoor was a bit emotional and asked him if everything was alright.

"I'm fine, I just revealed to my wife I think I am a Christ believer."

"Have you been reading more of the Bible?" Michael asked with a smile in his voice.

"I have boss and even more books about Jesus, historical references as well."

"It's important that you know that all his apostles were frightened to be killed after his crucifixion on the cross, afraid to even be seen on the streets. On the third day, when he rose from the dead, that all changed. His mission for them was simple: "Tell everyone about me and tell them I loved them so much I died to pay the price for the sins of all mankind." These very flawed and frightened men stepped outside into the light and began spreading the word of Jesus, regardless of what might happen to them. Most of them died horrible deaths, but never lost their faith in Jesus. Who would go to their death for a lie, Mansoor? You must now be extra careful because you will have a desire to spread the good news, but you may very well lose your life in the process. Anyway, I need you now. I need to know why Aqeel would go to Indiana?" Michael finally asked.

"He has turned a senator to help us infiltrate your very government. It came out as he bragged about how he would create destruction in your very halls of power." Mansoor told him.

"Keep reading, Mansoor, and I will find a way to get you and your family out of there," Michael said.

"God be with you, boss," Mansoor replied; then the phone went silent.

***

"Tess, who's the senator from Indiana that's getting all the attention?" Michael asked through the cell phone.

"That would be Grady Morrison. He's the new voice for the Democratic Party. He's quite a speaker." She said with a bit of admiration in her voice.

Michael picked up on it and said, "Don't get too excited about him because he's now on my hit list."

"You can't take out a senator, Michael. You've been going after bad men, but this guy hasn't done anything that would justify you killing him. It will be a line you cross and can never come back from. Please, you need to find a way to expose him to anything other than killing him. He is being considered a possible presidential candidate," she asked, almost pleading to change his mind.

"There is a poison infiltrating my country, and those in charge have become so corrupt and politically correct, they have turned a blind eye to this internal attack. I'm afraid some of those elected by the people have, in fact, become the enemy. They are holding tight to their position solely for the sake of re-election and the power and money it brings. This leaves me with no choice but to fight. If I find an American politician or his minion working to hurt America, I'll dissect him and leave his miserable carcass on the steps of the Capitol. Tess, this is how I wage war. My government only cared about results when I served in the jungles of Vietnam. I'm a soldier, and killing the enemy in war is what it's about, nothing more."

"But this isn't a war." Tess insisted.

"9/11 made it a war, and they drew first blood." He responded and then hung up the phone.

Chapter Seventeen: Nefarious

Michael sat in his car at Battery Park staring at the statue of Lady Liberty for a long time. He thought about his country and how much it had changed over the years. When he went to Vietnam, he felt he was surrounded by a country that supported his efforts. Upon his return, he was spat on as he walked through the airport terminal. It was something the protester would never forget. When the young man regained consciousness, he was instructed that he needed to go to the dentist to repair the damage to his front teeth.

Michael recalled music changing from themes about love to songs about getting high and letting go. These hippies, who were taught by liberal socialist professors in the colleges around the country, began to distrust the government that protected them. They were okay with peace without victory. They wanted change and lost respect for the government that every other nation in the world envied.

The politicians he had looked up to were being brought down by a press that saw scandal in everything he grew up believing in. He thought about all the assignments he had taken part in that helped the black man in America move closer to equality. He watched as his heroes were cut down in the prime of life by an unseen power that wanted to control everything. He had fought the good fight, cried with the thousands who lost loved ones on 9/11, and here he was preparing to make his way to Indiana and terminate the life of a sitting senator who compromised his moral code and betrayed his oath to the Constitution solely to gain power. Michael was disgusted with it all but knew that, regardless of how horrible he might look in the eyes of the populace, he had to finish the mission. This was getting ugly, and the more he infiltrated the terrorist faction, the more disgusting layers he discovered.

The trip would take over ten hours and cover over 728 miles of the America he fought for so long ago. Michael would pass through the town where he was born and raised by Italian immigrants who wanted nothing more than to give their children a better life. They endured starvation and the ravages of war in their Italian village of Manduria. They promised each other that if they survived, they would go to America, where anyone could start with nothing but a few dollars in their pocket and become anything they desired if they had the will to try in the face of adversity. His mind was recalling his own childhood and all his parents had given him. He instinctively pulled off the expressway and found the cemetery where those he loved were buried.

The headstones were surprisingly clean. He looked down and read out loud their names. "John and Mary Angelino together in life and together forever." He turned to the second stone, which was that of his incredible wife of thirty-two years. He knelt in front of it and prayed for God to guide him into the dangerous journey he was on and thanked Him for taking Elizabeth away before she had to see The Machine resurrected. "Elle, I guess you know I got married to Tess. She's a great gal, and she loves me almost as much as you. I only wish I could offer her what you and I had for so many years, but I think she will be placing me near you sooner rather than later. I still love you more than life, Elle. I'll probably be seeing you soon." He rose up and quickly made his way back toward the freeway. He made a quick stop at Walmart to get a digital recorder. Then back onto the freeway.

His cell rang. "Hello, sweetheart." He said, knowing it was Tess.

"I didn't like the way our last call ended." She acknowledged.

"Me neither, but for now I need you out of my head, or you might be attending my funeral, and I'm really not ready to call it a day." He replied.

"Understood. For now, just let me say I love you and want you to come home, preferably in one piece." Tess said, aware that this conversation would be short.

"I love you back, big time. I'll make contact when it's done." He clicked off and was about to cut off the phone when it rang again. He looked at the number, and it was his informant, Mansoor.

"What have you got for me?" Michael asked.

"Naqeem Kahn is a name that keeps getting spoken here. The leadership says he is the solution to your problem. I am unfamiliar with him, but as I learn more, I will be in touch," he whispered into the phone.

Michael could hear the sounds of cars and people in the streets, which made him feel a bit better about his source's awareness of the danger he was in. "Thank you, Mansoor. You must be very careful from now on. By the way, how is the search for truth coming along?"

"I'm glad you asked me because my beautiful wife and I have said the sinner's prayer and now follow Jesus, our Lord and savior. We continue to pray as directed by Islam, but instead we pray to Jesus and ask for his protection because to openly express our newfound faith could mean death." He explained to Michael.

"When I have completed this mission, I am coming to get you and your family out of there. Your work with me will be finished.

Do you understand? I'm telling you to get ready to travel. Start now. Understood?" He was emphatic in his tone.

"Yes! I understand, it will be done. Christ be with you. I must go and tell my love. Thank you, Boss." The phone became silent.

Michael spoke silently to God, It looks like some good is coming from all this hate, but that's your way, too, isn't it. No matter how we make lemons with our world, you find a way to make lemonade out of what we perceive as chaos. That's why I love you so much. Please be with me as I move forward.

Driving long distances sometimes makes a soldier think about things, and Michael was doing a lot of it. His journey took him past many American flags as he crossed over Pennsylvania and Ohio; the flag he fought for was honored and defended over the years. He thought about the national anthem and the man who wrote it. He found himself reciting the words out loud.

"Oh, say, can you see, by the dawn's early light,

What so proudly we hailed at the twilight's last gleaming?

Whose broad stripes and bright stars, thro' the perilous fight,

O'er the ramparts we watched, were so gallantly streaming?

And the rockets' red glare, the bombs bursting in air,

Gave proof thro' the night that our flag was still there.

O say, does that star-spangled banner yet wave

O'er the land of the free and the home of the brave?"

Michael loved the lyrics that spoke of American fortitude in the attack on Fort McHenry by the British in September 1814. Francis Scott Key, an attorney and amateur poet sent by order of the President to secure the release of Key's friend Doctor William Beanes, was on an American ship in the harbor as the British bombarded the stronghold all through the night. Upon seeing the symbol of his country still waving above the fort, Key was brought to tears, sat down, and wrote the poem that one hundred and seventeen years later would become the national anthem.

The Machine thought about how many brave men lost their lives for the belief that all men should be free to live their lives without the tyranny of a government dictating their future. What happened to his country, where men fought and gave their lives for our way of life? It was being replaced by young men indoctrinated into believing their college professors that America was bad and deserving of all the terrible things that were happening to them. When did the needs of the few outweigh the needs of the many?

The more he thought while driving, the angrier he became; until the monster he left in the jungles of Southeast Asia, became alive in him once more. His mission was clear; he needed only to find and eliminate his target.

Senator Morrison made his way to his car when The Machine caught a view of him downtown. He was heading to his beautiful home on Diamond Pointe Drive, followed by The Machine, who remained some distance behind on Interstate 70 heading east out of the metropolis. He watched the car move onto the 465 North. Michael looked at his watch, and fifteen minutes had passed. The senator's car moved onto the 36 East, and five miles later, he turned left on Oaklandon Road. He traveled about three miles and turned on Admirals Pointe Drive and made a quick left, 200 feet later, a right into his driveway. Michael honked his horn as he quickly pulled alongside the Senator in his triple-wide driveway.

"Senator, please get in the car." The Machine said firmly, the 9-millimeter pointed at his head.

"What is this about?" he asked as he opened the door to his car. "Do you have any idea who I am?"

"Yes, sir, I do. You should know that I am the man who has killed the terrorists in the Philippines and, most recently, killed terrorists in New York who were planning to crash another plane into the Sears Tower in Chicago. So, unless you would like me to kill your children and wife in front of you, I suggest we talk privately. I really don't want to involve your family." He answered politely.

"Alright, but you don't have to point that gun at me, do you?" he asked indignantly.

"We're just going to take a ride out to that new construction site down the street." He responded.

"Should I be concerned? I haven't done anything to deserve this." The senator was nervous about this man.

Michael wanted to get as much information from him before he decided on the final outcome of the conversation. He needed a bit more information to make the pieces fit. Who was Naqeem Kahn? Michael was replaying his wife's plea not to kill a senator.

The car pulled into the deserted housing development between two partially constructed homes. He turned off the engine and stared at the black man who moved so quickly up the ranks of the

Democratic Party, his 9mm held in his lap. His other hand gently pressed the record in his pocket.

“I want to know when you sold out and, more importantly, why?” The Machine’s cold eyes emphasizing his words.

“There are people in our country who believe that the world should be governed by one group, and in doing so, we could eliminate wars and international conflicts. I subscribe to this belief.” The senator pontificated.

“Senator, when you took office, you swore an oath to the Constitution, but you have broken that solemn promise. It is the same promise that soldiers have died to protect for over 200 years, and for breaking that promise, you must be held accountable.”

“Accountable to whom? A bunch of soldiers who follow orders, to a document written two hundred years ago. Wake up, man. There’s a new world order that is already moving into position. Congressman and Senators unable to pass the most common-sense bills is a way of getting the people of this country to turn their back on the old ways.” He said emphatically.

“Are you telling me there is an effort to dissolve the very laws that have made us the greatest country in the world?” Michael was pulling the information out of him because the narcissist was so self-righteous that he believed he was right.

“Who is Naqeem Kahn?” Michael asked.

“Kahn is a very rich businessman, along with many others who are already running the world.” The senator replied unashamedly.

“What did they promise you for your loyalty?” Michael already suspected the answer, but he needed to hear it.

"The presidency." He answered proudly.

"Puppets don't really have intelligence; they just respond to how the strings are moved," Michael said gently, then raised his weapon and sent three projectiles through the traitor's head.

He dragged the dishonored carcass from his vehicle. He thought to himself, If I'm lucky, the crows and blackbirds will feast on his remains before he's discovered. He took the small tape recorder and placed it in the senator's coat pocket. He got back into the car and began his trip back to Washington, D.C., then decided to get a bit of rest first. He drove to Steubenville, Ohio, and checked into the Hampton Inn. He knew that the Franciscan University was there, so once he settled into the room, he drove there to have a conversation with God. A few students are always in the chapel. Michael got on his tired knees and prayed…

I will be marked for death because of this act, but I just couldn't let him try to talk his way out of this. It needs to come to the surface, so America wakes up, Lord. Forgive me for my sins, for which there are many.

The following morning, Michael called Tess for information on the whereabouts of Aqeel Gabany. The cell phone rang, but no one picked up. Michael thought that it was highly unusual for her not to answer right away, but decided to just let it go. He needed to concentrate on his next assignment, which was to get Aqeel Gabany. If he survived that, perhaps he and Tess could get some R and R. He thought again about just killing a senator and thought to himself, who am I kidding?

Chapter Eighteen: Peremptory

The New York papers were having a field day ridiculing the police department for allowing a crazed vigilante to run loose in the city. They went out of their way to detail the viciousness of the attacks, followed by a quote from Imam Nader Nadershahi from the Long Island Mosque. “What can be gained by this horrible bloodshed but more of the same?” Detective Jaeger announced that his police were running every lead to determine who was responsible.

***

Tess looked down at her phone, but was in the middle of a meeting with the brass about this vigilante or group of vigilantes who were crisscrossing the globe killing Muslims. The President was directly overseeing the matter and was being briefed daily by the FBI. However, there was very little progress in identifying the person or persons involved. The only person who had anything to share with the FBI was Det. Roger Jaeger, who received a call from the person who mutilated the body of Robert Ellis. He spoke from New York by telephone.

“This could not be the work of one person. We believe whoever did this is part of a team of mercenaries who are acting as one unit with some very good intelligence. All the persons murdered were part of a terrorist cell with plans to fly planes into the Sears Tower in Chicago. We found plane tickets as well as a flight simulator program on their computer. Your people are going through the thing as we speak.” Roger said confidently.

"Thank you, Detective Jaeger. We appreciate the NYPD's assistance in this effort. We'll call again if we need further information, and of course, you'll send any forensic evidence that might identify any of these killers. Correct?" Tess inquired.

"Absolutely, we're on it, Ms. Lamia," Jaeger responded.

"Thanks again, Roger. Goodbye. Tess ended the group call and turned to those assembled in front of her.

"I believe our investigation needs to begin pulling the records of known ex-patriots who believe that the government isn't capable of handling the terrorist threat to the United States. My agents will follow up on all persons of interest. Is there anything else to discuss, gentlemen?"

"No, Tess. Excellent job." Ted Hobson said.

With that, the VIP's got up and left the conference room. Ted and Tess remained, and once the room was cleared, Ted turned to her and quietly asked, "Is it at all possible that Michael Angelino is still alive and on the loose?"

Tess reacted, surprised by the comment, and responded, "Ted, with due respect, you're out of your mind. Michael Angelino is dead. God rest his soul."

Tess's secretary, Shirley, came in flustered. "Ms. Lamia, Mr. Hobson, Senator Grady Morrison was just found dead, shot in the head. It's on the TV. Oh my God, this is just terrible."

"Oh no," Tess uttered under her breath.

"Tess, this vigilante group or Angelino has just crossed the line, even though I think he's dead too; this guy's history makes him a prime suspect," Ted said abruptly.

Ted hit the intercom, “I want everyone looking for this group of vigilantes, and put Michael Angelino on a person of interest list and send his photos out to all agents.”

“Ted, Michael is dead. This is just a waste of time.” Tess said emphatically.

“Tess, we'd better cover our ass?” Ted responded and left the room.

Tess looked down at her phone and realized she needed to warn her new husband that the dogs were being released. She dialed and waited through two rings.

“Good morning, sweetheart,” Michael said cheerfully.

“Ted has put you back on the person of interest list. I told him you were dead, but he’s freaking out that you or some crazy group of American NRA zealots is responsible for the death of the senator and everything else. The police in New York said you must be a group of avengers that one person couldn’t have caused all that carnage. “Senator Morrison Michael, you had to kill him?” she questioned in frustration.

“Tess, he was bad, and they were using him as a pawn for bigger things in the future. He had to be eliminated. I put an incriminating tape into his suit pocket. Your people will put the pieces together.”

“How are you going to get around? Your face will be on every field agent’s cell phone.” Tess was frightened for Michael.

“It will be alright, Hon. Don’t worry, I’ll be extra careful? I called for any information on Gabany.”

"I had a few agents watching him, but he caught a flight to Iran thirty minutes after the news broke about Morrison," Tess told her husband.

"No way to hold him, right? He queried.

"For what reason, Michael? He isn't even on the FBI or CIA radar right now. You are." She said, trying to emphasize the importance of what she was saying to him.

"He'll be heading for Teran, and that's where I'll end him." The Machine informed her.

"Be careful over there. I can provide you with some assistance if you need it; CIA assistance." She mentioned knowing he'd say no.

"I work better alone, and I'm not on their radar yet, just another face in the crowd, but thanks, Babe." He said sincerely.

She was about to tell him one more time she loved him, but the phone went dead. Tess knew that he was getting in the zone and that only killing would be on his mind.

Michael needed to get to Iran, but didn't want to use public airlines for fear that he might be recognized through facial recognition software that was just newly being used by the FBI. It was pretty accurate, and even though he had lost weight, he couldn't take the chance that he wouldn't be identified by it. He would have to find another way.

His mind began to evaluate his options. He thought about the Imam in Brooklyn and decided that this man might have rich donors to the mosque who might be able to assist him. He made his way there and went in to speak to Nader.

"I understand that you need to go to help your friend Ben, but why do you need to travel so secretly?" The Imam questioned.

"I have been questioned by the local FBI regarding what has happened recently. It appears that the minute it is known that you are a Muslim, you become a suspect in all things regarding terrorism. I was in the hotel where the young American was found dead, and I am now being watched. They told me not to leave town, but my friend needs my help, and I must get there to help him." Ben explained to the Imam.

"I have a friend of the mosque who is an international envoy for an Iranian diplomat. He travels back and forth almost three times a month. He is in town this week. I will give him a call and see if he can help." Nader explained to Ben and picked up the phone from his desk.

A few minutes later, he hung up and told Ben to go to Teterboro Airport on Highway 1 in New Jersey, just across the George Washington Bridge, the following morning, as the jet would be leaving from there approximately at ten.

"Ben the Jet's numerical marking is N610MS, and my friend Amir Bijan says you are welcome to join them," Nader explained.

Upon hearing the name Bijan, Michael recalled the dentist he tortured and beheaded in the dental chair in Galveston, Texas, and wondered how common the name was in the Middle Eastern culture. Michael shook his hand with both of his and thanked him repeatedly. Nader put his hand to Michael's face and said, "I can tell you are a good man, Ben; your friend is very lucky."

They said goodbye to each other, and Michael went back to his apartment to put his belongings together. He secured his 9-

millimeter and 380 weapons with four clips for each, holding hollow-point rounds in an overnight bag with a battle dress uniform in black, black camouflage paint for his face, black tactical gloves, and black tennis shoes. He put a pair of Levi's and two V-neck tee shirts on top. He wore a pair of Levi 501's, a T-shirt, and a light jacket over it. The jacket was for holding two magazines and a handgun if the occasion called for it. The morning would come soon enough, and Michael was getting psychologically ready for war. The last thing to get was a rifle with a high-power scope that could be disassembled and secured without detection. Michael's FBI experience taught him where he might just find such a weapon.

He drove into the city and met with a pawn shop owner. His name was Jason Gregory, and he was a Vietnam vet who had lost a leg in the conflict. Michael introduced himself as David Devlin and told him he was on a special assignment as an independent operative whose job was to take out a terrorist leader in Iran.

The ex-soldier smiled and said, "You came to the right place, my man."

He disappeared for a few minutes, then came back with a briefcase and placed it on the counter. Seeing the briefcase, Michael appeared disappointed.

Jason responded with a very wide smile on his face. "What is in the case is an all-plastic high-powered rifle weighing 3.2 pounds with a 5-12x42 scope with a laser for accuracy and a silencer. It resides under a false bottom and is totally undetectable from x-ray machine inspection, but you'd better be a good shot because this weapon is not designed for amateurs. You can only get three shots before the plastic gets hot. If you get off a fourth shot, it melts from the heat generated by the weapon. So, only use it in three-shot sequence, after which it needs at least fifteen minutes to cool off before using it again." The veteran store owner said as a matter of fact.

Michael was extremely impressed. "I think this will work for me. How much?" He asked.

"Eight hundred should do nicely." Came the response.

Michael dropped a thousand on the counter, looked at the soldier, and said, "I was never here. Right?"

"You got it, man." He said, giving a half-assed salute.

Michael was ready for another war zone. This time, deep within enemy territory. He looked towards Heaven and asked, "I hope you're still with me because this is going to get ugly fast." Michael didn't wait for an answer.

Chapter Nineteen: Circumvention

"Good morning, Mr. Bijan, I'm Ben Santana. Nader told me you would be able to get me to Tehran." Michael said, shaking the stranger's hand.

"Please call me Amir. I'm happy to help. How many days will you need, because I'm scheduled to return in a week?" Amir asked his new passenger.

"That should be fine. I feel a bit uncomfortable asking this, but is there any chance we can bring my friend and his family back with us?" Michael queried.

Amir was a bit curious and asked Michael why that would be necessary and how many people they were talking about. Michael thought for an instant and answered quickly.

"My friend Mansoor was injured, and the medical expenses have depleted the family bank account. I told him that if I were able, I would help defray some of the costs and have him seen here in the States by specialists. At the same time, I would like to take his wife and the twins to Disney World in Florida. If you provide the airfare, it would be all we need to have enough funds to make the trip. It's a once-in-a-lifetime opportunity for his boys, and he really requires good medical care."

The story was so innocent in nature that Amir bought it and, smiling, said, "I do not very often get the chance to make dreams come true. I'm happy to assist you. By the way, how old are his sons?"

"They're almost five, and that's how old my son was when I took him the very first time. He still remembers it." Michael lied with a broad smile.

During the fourteen-hour flight, Michael chatted with his host, telling him he had never visited Iran, but that he had converted to the Muslim faith. He had a fervent desire to make a pilgrimage to Mecca. His host described the holiest site in all Islam, the Al-Masjid al-Haram in Saudi Arabia, and that it was over two thousand miles from Tehran.

"That's much farther than I thought." He said, surprised.

"If I get instructions to go there as an emissary, perhaps you might be able to come along," Amir suggested with a smile.

"Your kindness is beyond words," Michael answered.

"We should rest a bit, and I'll have them prepare a light meal just before we arrive," Amir remarked as he grabbed the small pillow for his head.

"Great, I want to be as rested as I can before we get there. I'm so excited, I'm sure I won't sleep the first night there." Michael responded.

Michael closed his eyes and remembered an assignment in 1979. He was detailed to protect a foreign dignitary. It turned out to be the Shah of Iran who arrived in October to be seen by American doctors who specialized in cancer. Ten months earlier, the monarch was forced to leave Iran.

In 1975, the Shah abolished a multi-party system with a single party called the Rastakhiz (Resurrection) Party. This political move caused religious zealots to begin a civil unrest, which resulted in the

1979 revolution and the power grab by the once-exiled Ayatollah Khomeini. During that revolution, supporters of the Shah were hunted down and killed by the hundreds. The new regime would be based on the Ayatollah's harsh religious beliefs, which sent women's rights back to the dark ages and made Shariah law the way of life in Iran.

The Shah told Michael stories of a modern Iran that reflected the West in dress and culture. Women wore the latest fashions and men treated them as equals. The Shah had restructured the once third-world country into a thriving enterprise, but with the Ayatollah's rise to power, all that came to an end. Instead, the Western world was despised and became an enemy to the new Iran, and women became sub-citizens. The images became hazy as sleep overpowered the memories.

The sound of clinking glasses and silverware woke him. Amir was looking at him and smiling. "You sleep hard, Ben, like you don't get much."

"I haven't slept well worrying about how this miracle could happen for my friend, but I don't remember when I've gotten a better rest." Michael smiled back at his host.

"We're getting close, Ben. Look at my incredible city."

Michael viewed a huge modern city as the small jet made its way to the IKA (Imam Khomeini International Airport). It was a vast metropolis with an estimated 8.8 million people and reminded Michael of flying over Mexico City, except the modern buildings looked more like Chicago or New York. The plane began its approach and landed in an area away from the main terminal. Amir was an envoy, so from his plane, he and Ben Santana were not directed to the normal passenger passport zone, but upon arrival, they had an individual who reviewed and stamped passports as part of the white glove treatment for important diplomats and executives who flew in and out from around the world to do business.

"Where will you be staying, Ben?" Amir inquired.

"I really haven't made plans," Ben answered.

"I usually stay at the Espinas Palace Hotel. Let me arrange for you to have a room for the time you'll be here."

"I couldn't, Amir, you are too kind," Ben told him.

"Don't be silly. I insist. My expense account is quite lavish, as you say. Perhaps invite your friend and his family for dinner one night." Amir loved being a gracious host to his country, and this made him so happy.

"Thank you so much. You are so generous." Ben accepted with great humility.

The taxi ride through the city became a private tour as Amir pointed out important landmarks like the Milad Tower from the Tehran freeway, and closer to downtown, the Shah Abdul Azim Shrine. The trip took an hour and seventeen minutes, and Michael made mental notes of the trip.

The twenty-one-story hotel really looked like a palace once Michael came through the front lobby. Bell men dressed in red coats and black pants accented with gold buttons and trim were in uniforms that looked luxurious. Alabaster floors that were so shiny, they were illuminated by the lights from the four-tiered chandelier suspended from the center of a beautiful mosaic dome. The front desk clerk, upon seeing his American passport, tapped his bell, and he was immediately escorted to the seventeenth floor to room 1703.

Upon entering, there were two queen-size beds with crisp white sheets semi-covered with a gold cover and matching pillow cases. Michael thanked his guide and, once gone, made his way to the window. The view of the vast metropolis was almost too much to take in. Beautiful in the most cultural way, the architecture that manifested the design of Persia. He pulled out his cell phone and called Mansoor, who answered after one ring.

"Can you talk?" Michael asked.

"I can boss," Mansoor answered.

"I'm here in Tehran at the Espinas Palace Hotel. I've made arrangements to have you and your family transported by private jet back to New York City." Michael announced.

"Aqeel is here, and he is out of his mind with rage. He is suspicious of everyone, but I think especially me. He keeps asking me why I was allowed to live through the massacre in the Philippines. Today, he said, Why didn't they just kill you and post a message on your chest? I didn't have an answer for him except to pledge my loyalty to our jihad, but I don't think he believes me anymore."

"Where can I find him?" Michael asked.

"He is at his office in the city at 12 Emam Khomeini now, but leaves shortly for his apartment on Gheytarieh Boulevard in the north of Tehran. It's right around the corner from the International Fair. If you take the subway one north, the last stop is Gheytarieh. His address is G-1, but he has bodyguards with him at all times, two very large men who carry weapons." Mansoor described.

"Your family has been invited this evening to dinner by our host, Amir Bijan. It is at seven. I will be there, but I need to do some preliminary surveillance of his apartment." Michael told his informant.

Michael followed Mansoor's detailed instructions until he was a block away from G-1. He was in his Machine mode as he surveilled the area around the apartment. He watched for police and military so as not to cause suspicion. Michael took mental notes of the apartment layout from outside. He memorized window locations, the front door, as well as a fire exit from the back. His timing was so important, so he waited until just before dusk. It was a quarter after five, and a black Mercedes pulled up to the front of the apartment. Michael watched as two bodyguards escorted Aqeel into his home. The Machine watched as the two men inspected each room. Once this was done, Aqeel went into his room, and the two bodyguards went into the kitchen to fix themselves something to eat. It was apparent that this was a regular occurrence, so Michael would use the regularity to his advantage. He watched as one of the men began to cook on the stove, and shortly after, opened the window, probably to cool down the room.

The Machine opened his briefcase and quickly assembled the rifle. Darkness had replaced the light, and the laser pinpointed his targets. The man by the stove slumped forward, knocking the pan to the kitchen floor. The other man thought his partner had a heart attack and got up from his chair, only to fall forward on top of the other man. The back of his head exploded, leaving blood splatter all over the wall. There was no sound of glass breaking because they had opened the window, and the amount of noise the bodies made was only enough to make Aqeel yell down from his room to quiet down.

Michael fired one more shot from across the street, this time into the door itself. He ran, kicking the door open and closing it just as quickly. Aqeel appeared at the top of the stairs and ran back to his room. Michael, his 9mm out with a silencer, followed, kicking open the bedroom door as Aqeel placed a handgun into his mouth. Michael's weapon fired, putting a hole in Aqeel's hand and sending the pistol flying across the floor. Aqeel screamed like a little girl, but only once as Michael struck him in the head. While unconscious, Michael hog-tied the terrorist mastermind, making movement in any direction impossible, but just to be extra safe, he tied him to the bed as well. It was six fifteen in the evening, and Michael had a dinner engagement. So, feeling comfortable with his new captive, he left and caught the subway back to the hotel. A quick change into evening wear, and he made his way down to the first floor, where he saw a familiar face standing next to their host, Bijan.

"Mansoor, how are you, old friend?" Michael said and whispered into his ear as they embraced. "Call me Ben. I have Aqeel."

Mansoor turned to his family, "Ben, you remember my wife Adiva and my boys Jaazar and Jaaziel."

"Yes, of course." He turned to Adiva and said, "As-Salam-u-alaikum."

Adiva bowed gently and responded, "Wa alaykum as-salam."

"My goodness, your children have grown since our last visit. They are the perfect age for a trip to Disney World." Michael intended to lay a foundation.

With that, Mansoor turned to Bijan and thanked him again for the use of his plane. Bijan bowed with a smile and said, "Ben told me about your injuries. If you go with the family to Disney World, you should use a wheelchair." Then looked at the boys and said, "It will be faster to get on the rides. Shall we go to dinner?" Everyone nodded.

During the meal, Michael described Disney World to the twins. As Adiva translated, all could see the eyes of the boys grow large with wonder at such a magical place. Their excitement was obvious.

The dinner was a wonderful collection of Middle-Eastern delicacies in five courses ending with a tray of Basbousa, a delicate sweet cake with coconut; Baklava, a rich sweet filo dough layered with pistachios and dripping with honey; and Oumm Ali (Ali's mother), a bread pudding with a cinnamon nut filling. When dinner ended, Adiva excused herself and the twins so the men could discuss more adult issues.

The men enjoyed strong aromatic coffee while Amir described the wonderful job he had working for a wealthy businessman who was part of the government. This sparked Michael's interest because he wondered if Amir was working for someone Morrison talked about.

Mansoor was very good at working the ruse with their host, and Bijan was very much enjoying the evening and the company. They avoided conversation about politics and terrorism and instead focused on Michael's conversion to Islamism. Michael's explanations and personal journey to the faith were an exciting string of lies that brought tears to Mansoor and Bijan.

Bijan's phone rang. "Excuse me, Gentlemen, I must take this, it is my employer."

The two men listened as the phone conversation appeared to be heated. Bijan could be heard saying, "As you wish, sir." Upon his return to the men, he stated that he would be leaving for New York earlier than expected, as his employer had a last-minute business meeting come up that required him to travel to California.

Michael was glad for the change in plans because there were dead bodies that would eventually be found, and he preferred being gone when they were discovered. He turned to Mansoor and asked, "Can you be ready sooner?"

"I believe we can be, but I'll check with my wife, although I believe she has already taken care of the boy's clothes and things. Yes, I'm sure we'll be ready."

"Wonderful! So sorry for the inconvenience, but as long as it works out for everyone, we're on for departure tomorrow at one p.m.," Bijan announced happily.

The three men shook hands. Bijan took the elevator up to his room. Mansoor told Michael he would prepare his wife for the change in plans. Michael told his informant that he would be working to get information from Aqeel. Upon hearing that, Mansoor winced, recalling how Michael got information out of him. He left Michael by the elevator, met up with his wife and children, and went home, thinking to himself, Tomorrow will be the last time I will be home.

Chapter Twenty: Killing Rationale

Michael arrived back at Aqeel's apartment by taxi and found the mastermind sweating and breathing heavy with exhaustion from trying to get free of his bindings. He got down on the floor in front of his captive and quietly asked for information about Khan. He took the gag from his mouth and allowed Aqeel to speak.

"I will not tell you anything. You're going to kill me anyway." With that, he spat at Michael.

"How you die depends on how much information I get from you," Michael explained. He gagged Aqeel and went into the kitchen, where he found a cutting block with a variety of blades in it. He took a cleaver and a serrated blade and returned to the room.

Aqeel looked up and saw the knives. Michael got back on the floor and softly said, "One blade will be like a saw, it will take a long time to get through all the tissue and bone before I'm done, which will hurt like hell, or I can use the cleaver, which will be much quicker and hurt a lot less. Who is Naqeem Kahn?" He removed the gag.

"Fuck you," Aqeel yelled at him.

"Wrong answer, Aqeel." The Machine said quietly.

The gag was placed in his mouth, and the serrated blade began sawing through his pinky finger. Aqeel screamed in agony through the entire ordeal.

Michael said, "The sad thing is that I already knew who Khan is. That was just to see how much pain you were willing to endure.

What I want to know is, what is his next target? Shall we try again?" He removed the rag from his mouth.

"Yes, I will tell you (panting with pain), but first tell me where the rest of your men are?" Aqeel asked, short of breath.

"I will answer you, Aqeel, if only to make you see how very futile your jihad is. There is only me. I hit the team in Galveston. I made the mess in Mexico City. I found out about your attack on the Governors in California, and I killed them all. I went after Zafeer in the Philippines, and the terrorist camp was destroyed by me. I found out about your plan to destroy the subway in London, and kill one team and had the others arrested. I would have killed Avery myself, but his guilt got to him. I found out about your proposed destruction of the Sears Tower, and your suicide squads in New York were all killed by me. Oh yes, your special senator Morrison was also killed by me. Now, where will Kahn attack next?"

Aqeel was staring at a killing machine who he now knew was capable of anything, and he knew he was going to die a horrible death just like he was promised. "There will be many attacks in many places by jihadists willing to give their life for the killing of as many infidels as they can. Do what you will to me. I won't tell you anything else. Let's see how long you last with no information about the next attack. You can't be everywhere."

Michael thought to himself Lord, I'm not going to get anything from him, and I am so tired of all the torture.

He looked Aqeel in his eyes and said, "The God of Jacob and Abraham and our Messiah and Lord Jesus Christ, the son of the living God, has sent me to destroy your jihad, and unfortunately, you will not be there to see it."

Michael pulled out his 9mm with a silencer attached and placed it on Aqeel's forehead. Aqeel's mouth fell open in the realization that his life was about to end. Michael pulled the trigger three times, exploding the terror-monger's brains all over the wall behind him.

Michael slowly got up and walked from the house. He went only a block and found a taxi, which took him back to the hotel.

***

Every news media outlet was quick to report the assassination of Senator Morrison before anyone had all the information. In the age of a twenty-four-hour news cycle, getting the story right was replaced with getting it first. The black religious leaders of the country were calling it racism, calling for investigations, and demonizing all white America. The liberals were beating their collective chests, begging for answers and declaring the conservatives responsible for the hateful way blacks have been treated for the past two hundred years. The ignorant youth used the murder as an excuse to riot and plunder their local merchant stores, breaking glass windows and burning parked cars to show their disgust with their country, all the while stealing televisions, CD players, cell phones, or anything they could get their dirty hands on. The college professors who hate the country that gave them tenure used the killing of the senator as a way of bringing their message of a socialist form of government as the cure-all for the country. The politicians demanded more security in one breath and gun control in the second breath. The Senator's wife was interviewed, telling the country she was never more ashamed of America.

***

At the office of the terrorist task force, Tess Lamia and Ted Hobson were attempting to line up all the dots to get a clear picture of what happened. Tess knew but needed Ted to come up with the answers. If she gave any hint of knowledge about the killing, it would solidify Ted's suspicions about Michael Angelino. Local agents in Indiana found the recorder in the Senator's pocket that clearly implicated him with known terrorists, and his bank account was being audited by agents of the FBI who specialize in terrorist financial activity. Hobson was not yet ready to release the information regarding an ongoing investigation, but the hasty news media was only causing more hysteria. He decided to leak a story that the slaying could have something to do with a terrorist cell, thereby adding to the onslaught of erroneous reporting. Reporters content with printing unsubstantiated tripe would continue to spew rumors, while the few real journalists would be forced to do some old-fashioned investigating, which would give Hobson's department some time to put the pieces together.

Tess was working the terrorist angle but only mentioned Aqeel Gabany as a person of interest in regard to the murder, seeing no point in implicating Chet Avery. Her attention was on a name delivered to her by her new husband, and that was Naqeem Kahn. She was good at pulling up information from her computer, which had access to personal information on almost anyone in the United States, whether they were a citizen or not.

"One of my sources has come up with a businessman from Pakistan by the name of Naqeem Kahn." She announced to Ted, who had just walked into her office. She continued, "My source believes he is very involved, at least financially, in the recent terrorist activity."

"Good, keep me in the loop on that. I just came in to update you on the Morrison killing. It would appear a 9mm was used, but forensics has not been able to tie it to any previous shootings. There were no fingerprints, which suggests either a professional hit or one made to look like one. Our analysts have been combing over Morrison's financials, and it appears he has an offshore account in the Bahamas with over a hundred thousand dollars in it. Bank records also show he has a large bank deposit box at the same location. His wife says she doesn't know anything about such an account, but I'll bet she's lying. Oh, by the way, heard from Angelino?" Ted asked with a slight smile.

"Ted, let's not waste time on ghosts and get serious on real leads," Tess replied without looking up.

"Okay, you're right. On a more personal level, how is the marriage going?" Ted asked.

"David's gone a lot, but we're still getting used to his schedule. I think it will take some time, but you know, both of us have pretty busy lives and some adjustment is bound to be required." She responded.

"I'm not one who believes the heart grows fonder when people are apart, but I wish you luck, Tess, really I do," Ted said sincerely, but was hoping it wouldn't last.

"Thanks, Ted," Tess replied, but was inwardly thinking about all the recent events and wondering how or if Michael could make it back to her. It was only a matter of time before exposure would have him running for his life with both sides of the equation wanting him stopped or dead.

***

Across the Atlantic, a weary soldier rested on a luxurious hotel bed. His mind was overwhelmed dealing with an ideology that was committed to the destruction of America, and the far-reaching magnitude of it brought the soldier to his knees in prayer to the deity that gave him solace.

"Heavenly Father, your word has taught me to trust in you with my whole heart, my whole soul, and all of my mind. I love you, Lord, and will be okay with whatever happens to me. Not my will but yours be done. Amen." Moments later, Michael drifted off to sleep, exhaustion overtaking him completely.

Chapter Twenty-One: Questions

Mansoor was up by five in the morning and did as he always did, turning on his television for the news of the day. His color changed as he stared at the screen. The reporter was standing outside the home. Aqeel Gabany "Neighbors told authorities they heard some muffled high-pitched screaming in the night but heard no shots or even sounds of a struggle." He went on to describe a horrible murder inside. Mansoor immediately picked up the phone to call his boss. It rang only once.

"Hello, Mansoor, what's up?" Michael asked.

"Al Jazeera is reporting on Aqeel's death. Just a moment, someone is at my door."

Mansoor answered the door. Two police men asked if he was Mansoor Amoli. He told the officers he was. They told him he needed to go with them down to police headquarters. Michael was listening as the conversation continued.

"Why, what's the problem? Amoli asked.

"Your name has been implicated in the murder of Aqeel Gabany. Come with us now." The higher-ranked officer said sternly.

"May I let my wife know where I will be?" Mansoor inquired.

"You can call her from the station, and I'll take your phone," came the reply.

Michael knew this was trouble because his informant told him that Aqeel was becoming suspicious. The phone went dead, and

Michael was already putting on his clothes and heading for the door. He would need to get a visual of the police station, both inside and out.

They arrived at the principal police station in Tehran. There were rusted bars over the windows of the building. Once inside, Mansoor realized he had never been in a police station of any kind. The visibly shaken man was placed in a small cubicle. About ten minutes later, a tall man with a heavy mustache entered and introduced himself. "I am Mohammed Grober of the Gendarmerie. Do you know why you are here?"

"No, I was supposed to meet with Mr. Gabany this morning to discuss business," Mansoor told the detective.

"Was this a scheduled appointment?" Grober inquired.

"No, but it is not uncommon for me to come by to discuss things." Mansoor knew that they had his scheduled appointment book, so he recognized how he should answer to avoid further suspicion.

"I have a note written by the late Gabany that questions your loyalty. Where were you last night?" Grober questioned.

The detective lowered his head until he was face to face with his suspect, and before Mansoor could answer, he threatened, "You will be staying with us until I am satisfied that I can rule you out."

"I was with my wife and my boys at our home." He answered quickly.

The detective pulled out of his pocket the phone the officer had confiscated from him earlier and looked through his recent contacts. "Adiva, is she your wife?"

Mansoor nodded and said, “Yes, she is, sir.”

“Well, let’s just give her a call. Shall we?” He said as he pressed the call button.

After a few minutes, he heard a soft voice answer, “Mansoor, where did you go?”

“I’m Detective Grober of the Gendarmerie. Your husband is here under investigation for the murder of Aqeel Gabany. Where was your husband last night?”

“We had dinner with friends and then came home and went to bed.” She answered sincerely.

“What time did you go to bed?” was another question from the detective.

“It was about ten thirty.” She answered.

“So, after you fell asleep, you would not know if your husband left the house, would you?” Grober asked firmly.

“My husband is a good man. He and Mr. Gabany worked together and have known each other for years. He would never hurt him.” She professed earnestly.

“Your husband will be here for some time. Thank you for your information.” He said and turned off the phone.

He turned facing Mansoor and said, You will remain here until I am satisfied that you are not involved.” That said, the detective abruptly left the room.

***

Tess needs to be called. Michael thought to himself as he stepped into a taxi. “Take me to the Police headquarters.” Michael requested, and the driver took off.

He pressed her number on the phone and waited for the connection. “Hey Tess, are you available to talk?”

“Are you all right?” She asked, surprised by the call.

“Yes, fine. You sound out of breath.” He answered.

“I was soaking in the tub and left my cell on the bed.” She answered.

“Does that mean you’re naked and dripping wet by the bed?” He asked seductively.

“Yes, it does, but don’t get me started, you’re too far away.” She said with a giggle.

“Sorry about that, but I need a big favor from you. My informant is in danger here and needs asylum for himself and his family. We’ll be arriving in New York around eight or nine in the evening. Can you set it up?” Michael asked.

“Text me the names of each person, and I will get the paperwork started. Asylum takes about forty-five days for approval. What airport will you be coming in on?” She asked.

“Teterboro Airport, why?”

“I’ll be there,” Tess answered calmly.

“Be safe, Michael, and come home to me,” Tess stated warmly.

“I’ll do my best, babe. Talk soon.” Michael said and ended the call.

The taxi pulled up to the curb in front of the police station, and Michael paid the fare and thanked the driver. He got out and walked around the block to see all entrances and exits. Almost all the windows were decorated with bars over them. He noted that two on the side of the building next to the alley were not barred. He made a mental note of their location. After two trips around the building, he went inside.

"Good morning," Michael said to the desk officer.

The man's eyes got larger as he could tell by the language that this was an American. "Good morning, can I help you? The officer said in very broken English.

"Yes. My friend was brought here this morning for questioning, and I'm here to pick him up if they are done with him." Michael said.

"Just a moment." The clerk said. The officer picked up the phone and spoke in Iranian, then hung up. A moment later, Detective Grober opened the door. Michael saw a long hallway that appeared to extend to the end of the building with offices on the left and two small hallways on the right, which looked like they might be interrogation cubicles.

The detective introduced himself and asked what Michael's business was with Amoli.

"I was on the phone with him earlier when the officers picked him up, and his wife called me and told me that a detective Grober, who is you, asked her some questions about where he was last night. I guess I just thought that by now he should be ready to go back home, and I came to escort him as we only have a brief time together before I have to leave to go back to America."

"What is your business with Amoli?" He asked Michael.

"I represent Muslim mosques in New York that have been persecuted by the police and non-Muslim Americans, and Mr. Amoli has been very helpful in how to deal with the problem."

"Americans are afraid of anyone who is different from them." The detective asserted.

Michael said, "Yes, you're right."

"Mr. Amoli will be here for quite a while. I am afraid he is not being very cooperative. He said.

"May I speak with him for just a moment to discuss transporting his wife by car to her doctor's appointment and shopping for groceries?" Michael asked.

"Just for a moment," Grober said and reopened the door to the passageway.

Michael looked in both directions casually as they moved to the second hallway on the right. Grober opened the door of the first cubicle. Inside, Michael saw Mansoor looking a bit stressed.

"Assalamu Alaikum," Michael greeted the prisoner

"Wa alaykum assalaam," Mansoor responded.

"The kind detective said I could speak with you regarding your wife's doctor's appointment. May I use your car, and will Adiva be able to direct me?" Michael asked.

"Of course, you can, and yes, Adiva knows the way, even though she can't drive herself; she knows even the better roads to his office." Mansoor played along, knowing this man was already coming up with a plan for his escape.

"I will tell your wife you are alright. Let me know if you need me to pick you up later, whenever the detective is done with you. Okay?" Michael asked.

"I will contact you at his home, but it may be a day or two before I am satisfied with his answers. This is a murder investigation." The detective said and shut the door.

"Thank you for your kindness, sir," Michael said, all the while counting the heads of all the personnel that were visible from his perspective. The count was at twelve. He thought to himself, I have had worse odds, I'll just have to play it smart.

Once outside, he walked again around the building. The unbarred window was in the second hallway where Mansoor was being detained. He would park the car in the alley, kill all the officers, break the window, jump into the car, and race to the airport where his wife, kids, and Bijan would be waiting.

He caught a taxi to the hotel, secured all his gear, took a taxi over to Mansoor's residence, got his wife and boys, and brought them to the airport. It was eleven o'clock in the morning, and his timing would need to be exact to make the flight at one. His photographic mind was walking through the police station, with a plan to remove his informant and not get killed in the process.

Chapter Twenty-Two: The Dance

The clock said eleven forty-five in the morning. Michael pulled Mansoor's car into the alley adjacent to the second unbarred window. He put on black camouflage, including a mask, and went through the front door, where there were just a few people waiting to be seen. He pointed the silencer at the police clerk. "Open the door." The officer rose slowly, took his keys out with his fingertips to avoid being killed for moving too fast. Once the door was unlocked, the man in black struck him on the head, which knocked him out. An officer was coming out of the office on the left, and the weapon spat out silent death. Two other officers came out of Grober's office, closed the door, and were taken down by the intruder. The death dance was happening so quickly that it caught them all by surprise, with little time to react. The Machine moved into the second hallway on the right and entered the cubicle to find Mansoor praying.

"Keep praying, my friend, but let's do it in the car," Michael said lightly. He turned his weapon on the window and shattered it with one shot. He knew the noise would set off alarms, but trying to go back the way he came would be impossible, too many civilians in the way. Mansoor went out first and was thrown the keys to his car. Michael was on his way out when he heard Detective Grober trip over the bodies outside his door, and three policemen drew their guns to stop the man in black. Michael put his gun over his left shoulder and fired three rounds blindly. The bullets made contact, but nothing fatal; however, it was enough to drop them for the minutes he needed to get in the car.

“The airport is as fast as the car will go,” Michael ordered.

“My wife and the boys?” Mansoor was asking about them with concern.

“They’re already there and waiting for us,” Michael assured him.

The sound of sirens could be heard in the distance behind them, and they were coming up faster than he hoped. Michael took the plastic rifle with the high-powered scope and faced the rear of the vehicle. He had only four shots with this weapon, and he knew they had better count. Suddenly, a shot shattered the back window as the fastest police car gained on them. Michael aimed and fired one round into the driver’s front tire, which sent the car careening to the right, and a moment later, he could see an explosion as it struck a parked SUV.

The siren continued as Mansoor’s car got on the Persian Gulf Freeway. Mansoor sped past cars, weaving from the slow lane to the left side of the fast lane, avoiding traffic. As the sirens sounded, traffic pulled over to let the police car go through. Two police cars were now within 200 feet of their car, which was traveling at over ninety miles an hour. The plastic weapon came up again, this time it sent a bullet right between the driver’s eyes. He slumped forward, and his foot pressed down on the gas pedal. The car lunged forward, hit the tail end of the car in front of them, began to flip in the air, and came down, causing an explosion. The chase continued with two more police cars in pursuit. In the last car was Detective Grober, enraged that anyone could have the audacity to attempt an escape in broad daylight.

Michael and Mansoor were on the off-ramp for the airport that extended three kilometers to their terminal. Michael had two more shots with the disposable weapon, and he raised it to hit the car as it was coming off the freeway. This time, he hit the passenger front tire, and the car swerved to the left and crashed through the retaining wall on the off-ramp and dropped about forty feet, exploding on impact.

Mansoor drove to the departure area for private planes. The police car with Grober was moving in. Michael took the rifle one last time, aimed, and fired at the driver, but the weapon must have reached a maximum heat because it misfired. Michael pulled out his 380 and aimed carefully, firing eight shots into the police car. It accomplished its mission, killing two and wounding the remaining passenger, with the car coming to a stop right in the middle of the road.

Once they parked the car, Michael discarded the mask and gloves into a trash can inside the private terminal bathroom. Mansoor was excited to be reunited with his family. Bijan was curious why Ben was all in black, but decided to ask after they were off the ground and on their way back to the States. It only took ten minutes for them to show their papers and get on board the jet. When they entered, Bijan offered his guests champagne for the adults and soda for the boys.

The flight was the first time in too many hours for Michael to get some rest. He looked over at Adiva, holding on to Mansoor as he described his ordeal very quietly after the boys fell asleep. Bijan spoke briefly with Ben and asked why he was dressed the way he was. Michael proceeded to tell his host that he was asked by Mansoor to do a talk on terrorism at his office, and proceeded to lie about wanting to be an actor and showing up in costume to emphasize the talk. Bijan liked Ben and bought every bit of the story without question. After thanking Bijan for his incredible kindness,

Michael told him he would try to get a bit of rest. Bijan agreed to take his tiny pillow and lie back in the reclining seat.

In the darkness of the private jet, Michael spoke with God, thanked Him for allowing the soldier another day and for helping him bring a new Christian to safety.

Chapter Twenty-Three: Homecoming

Al Jazeera was reporting an extraordinary daytime attack at the Tehran police department, where a person of interest in a local murder was aided by American assailants, and a high-speed chase followed. Although outnumbered, the Tehran police made every effort to apprehend these foreign invaders; however, all attempts to capture them failed, and they escaped via a jet plane that was waiting for them at the international airport. Police detective Grober told reporters that the English-speaking intruders came in heavily armed, wounded many of his men, and escaped through a side window of the station. "Obviously, they were well prepared," Grober said to the reporter. More details as they become available.

***

In Washington, D.C., the incident was regarded as an attempt to further the propaganda of America's interference in the Middle East. The CIA was trying to find out what mercenary group might have been involved, while the President was denying any involvement in the attack. The town was abuzz with questions but no definitive answers. It was the typical unsubstantiated assertions that were a part of the Washington inner circle.

***

"How many men do you think Michael has working with him, Tess?" Ted Hobson asked as he walked into her office.

"Ted, stop beating a dead horse. Do you really think Michael could be involved in this? You told me his file said he was a loner who rarely worked with anyone and never was a part of a team. This report clearly states that a large group was involved." Tess stated with frustration in her voice. "This is CIA turf anyway, so let's get back to the cases in New York and Indiana. I really believe we're dealing with right-wing constitutionalists who have taken the law into their own hands." She concluded emphatically.

"Sorry, Tess, you're right of course. It's just hard to think of a soldier like Michael Angelino dead. It certainly appears that whoever this group is, they have access to a lot of confidential information." Ted said, scratching his head, and followed with, "They have more information than we do, and we're working with the CIA. So, who are these guys and what is the CIA not telling us?"

"Ted, let's stay focused on what's going on with Morrison. It would appear, based on the information they found on him, that he was working with a terrorist organization that has been funding him for some time. The big question is, where does the money lead us?"

Tess was trained extensively by the FBI on international financing, and their motto was always follow the money trail. Her expertise in this area proved fruitful. After just about half an hour on her computer, she came across the name Naqeem Kahn as a prominent businessman who donated a considerable sum of money to Morrison's latest campaign. After more digging, she found that this man was a regular contributor to Morrison. After reviewing the senator's campaign contributors, she found that Kahn had ties to several dummy organizations that also contributed the maximum amount to the senator's coffers.

Information about the man himself appeared to be sketchy, which made her gooseflesh rise. Tess knew she was on the right track because her husband had already mentioned his name, but she could not find an address for him in the United States. She did find an address in France in the heart of the financial district of Paris, known as La Defense. The address was Kahn Investment Management Services, Tour AXA, Suite 424. It was named after the AXA insurance company, which bought the building from the UAP insurance company. Many people photographed the building without even knowing it. The skyscraper sits tall within the financial district because the Eiffel Tower can be seen in front of it.

Tess brought the data into Ted's office. He went over the information and said, "It's pretty clear why you were so valuable to Angelino; this is magnificent work, Tess."

"Thanks, Ted, but we don't have anything on him to alert Interpol." She responded with frustration.

"I've got a contact, Jacques Dubois, at their headquarters, which just so happens to be in Lyon, France, which is only about four and a half hours from Paris by car or an hour by air. I'll ask him to make Kahn a person of interest." He told her with a wink.

Okay, Ted, keep me in the loop on this." Tess said and left the office. She turned back and popped her head in. "I'm going to take off early if that's okay. My husband is going to meet me later tonight, and I'd like to get cleaned up if you know what I mean."

"Sure, Tess, have a good night," Ted answered sincerely. She responded with a smile and shut the door.

Tess got into her car and made her way home to get pretty for her husband's return. She found an attractive outfit in her closet, one Michael hadn't seen her in. She took a long, hot shower and put on the clothing. She sprayed some Beautiful cologne into the air and walked into it; then she sprayed on one wrist and put her wrists together to even out the smell. Tess felt like she was going to her senior prom. She looked into the mirror to make sure she hadn't gotten any lipstick on her teeth and gave herself a final look. In her mind, she was singing, I am pretty, oh so pretty…. She looked at her watch. It was four thirty in the afternoon. Tess knew it would be just a bit over four hours to get to Teterboro Airport in New Jersey. She settled in behind the wheel, knowing that Michael would want to avoid commercial airports since Ted had put him on the person of interest list.

Tess needed quality time with her man, and once they were both satisfied, they would need to come up with a game plan moving forward. Her mind was racing as she made her way onto the Jersey Turnpike. Michael needs to disappear for a while. She thought to herself. Can I convince him that it would, in fact, be better for him to avoid combat somewhere? As long as Michael was in war mode, it would only keep Ted guessing that Michael was alive and actively creating international havoc everywhere he went. However, my last conversation with Ted made me feel I had dispelled any notion that my old boss was still alive; that and the fact that the latest report indicated a large contingency of men, which didn't sound like Michael's MO at all. It made me feel that perhaps the heat might be off, but I can't allow myself to take anything for granted because Michael's life hangs in the balance.

She was early. She picked up her cell phone and contacted the New York branch of the FBI to let them know they were needed to pick up a very important informant and his family, who escaped from Iran at the Teterboro Airport. Then she called Ted.

"Ted, I was getting ready for my husband's homecoming when I got an anonymous call telling me the informant who was rescued from the jail in Tehran was coming to New York. I've already contacted the New York branch to let them know, and I'm en route there now." She informed her boss.

"Did they give you any other information. Like who they are?" He asked.

"No, just to take care of them because the informant was assisting their cause and ours." She lied with believability.

"Did the group have a name?" He questioned.

"No. He did say that the poisoning of our political leaders could not be tolerated and that we needed to investigate all of them and root out all the bad apples. My husband called and isn't going to be home until tomorrow night, so I'm driving up to meet the plane. Perhaps this informant can provide more information about whoever the group is that saved him." She told Ted.

"Great Tess. I'll fly to New York in the morning. Just let me know where you take them, and I'll meet you there tomorrow." Ted said, his mind racing.

"Awesome, see you then. I'll text you with all the info." She answered him and then closed her cell.

Tess realized that by creating an entity of unknown forces, she could take even more pressure off her husband, and for Tess, that was priority one. She googled hotels near Central Park, picked the Courtyard, and called for reservations for two adjoining rooms with a view. She then called another hotel a couple of blocks away from the first and made a reservation for one room with a king-size bed. By the time all the arrangements were made, Tess had only a few minutes to say a prayer of thanks for her husband's safe return. She looked up and watched as a private jet landed and made its way to the small terminal. The passengers disembarked from the jet, and a moment later, she could see Michael. She watched from a distance as Michael shook hands with a gentleman who quickly made his way to a limousine and departed. Michael stood with a man, a woman, and two young boys. She phoned him from her car.

"I'm here." She said before he could say hello.

"I have a team from the FBI coming to take the family to a hotel in New York, and Ted is flying in to meet with them. The story is that I received a call from unknown forces who were responsible for this man's escape, and that they are a small contingency of Constitutionalists who are most likely ex-military or mercenaries. Please make sure your man has that story down pat because it was the only way to remove you from the equation."

"First, I love you; second, you're becoming as good a liar as I am, and third, what would you have me say to the FBI when they arrive?" He questioned sarcastically.

"Ha ha ha. I'm in the parking lot facing your location. Give the informant the story and make your way here. Once you get here, I'll kiss your face off. Then I'll make my way there and introduce myself to them. The FBI team should arrive within an hour. Stay in the car and keep low…just in case." She ordered him.

"Yes, ma'am!" he responded politely.

He closed the cell and sat with the family. After explaining what would most likely happen next, he took Mansoor aside.

"You are a child of God now, and you are in a country where you can speak freely about your relationship with God. Christ wants us to share the good news of the gospels, and you do that by loving your fellow man, not just with words but in your actions as well. Remember, Mansoor, for you, the war is over. I will soon go back into battlefields, so my friend, pray for me." Michael shook his hand and then embraced him. In the ten minutes it took to get to the parking lot, Michael was getting emotional because part of him envied the ex-terrorist and the new start he was given. When he got to Tess's car, she grabbed him and kissed him passionately, her hands on his face. She pulled away to look at him, then kissed him again.

"Okay, get in the car and relax for a while. I'll be back as soon as I can." She said and abruptly turned to leave, only took a step, and returned to him for another face-smashing kiss, then made her way to the same terminal area.

Tess flashed her badge to the TSA officer and made her way through the terminal to where the family was sitting. She immediately introduced herself to them, and they shook her hand.

Mansoor told her a team of military men rescued them, and a kind man brought them to America in his private jet.

"I understand, Mansoor. I have a detail from the FBI who will be arriving shortly and taking you into New York to stay in a wonderful hotel, and tomorrow you'll be meeting my boss, Ted Hobson, who has many questions for you. It is important that you tell him exactly what you told me. Do you understand?" Tess looked at the couple as she asked the question. Both he and his wife nodded.

"Let's go out to the main area where we'll wait for my officers to arrive." With that said, Tess escorted the family beyond the security checkpoint.

Michael watched from Tess's car and saw a pair of agents introduce themselves to Tess. Tess appeared to be giving instructions to the men, who nodded. They escorted the family to a large black van, and a few moments later, they were gone. Michael watched Tess walk quickly back to the car, admiring her beauty every step of the way.

When she got into the driver's seat, she immediately leaned over and kissed Michael again and again. The two got lost in the moment, smelling each other as they embraced. After about ten minutes, Tess filled him in on what would happen next.

"We'll be staying in a hotel near where they're taking Mansoor and his family. They're booked at the Courtyard in Midtown East. I picked it because it's close to the theatre district, Times Square, and Rockefeller Center. I even got them adjoining rooms 1614 and 1616 on the 16th floor with a view of Central Park. We're at the Fairfield Inn on 28th Street. It's only about two and a half blocks from them. You can hang out at our hotel while I meet Ted in the morning to make sure the family is on script about what happened. I'll make sure that we get them set up with immigration for expedited asylum status."

"He knows a lot about what's going on over there, and he could be in grave danger," Michael informed her to be aware.

"I've got this, babe. She assured him. "Only two people know he's arrived: Ted and the head of the New York office."

Tess pulled into the valet parking area of the Courtyard and told the attendant she wasn't staying, only going to check in some friends. He waved her an okay sign. Michael stepped out of the car to give the place a quick once-over. He chatted with the valet attendant. Tess returned about ten minutes later, and the two drove a few blocks away.

"Okay, they're safe and checked in, and I secured room 1615 across from them for the FBI agents. They will be relieved at midnight by another pair of agents." She said, feeling good about her attention to detail.

"Great," Michael replied. Deep inside, he was getting an uncomfortable feeling, but he kept it to himself.

They checked into their room, and as soon as the couple dropped their bags, they embraced and proceeded to undress each other. Michael was careful to gently unzip her dress and took the time to tell her how beautiful she looked in it. Tess was a bit more aggressive; she pulled off his shirt and started working on his pants. He stopped her, slipped them off, wrapped his hands around her back, and quickly unsnapped her bra. As she removed it from her shoulders, his hands removed her panties, and he dropped to his knees in front of her. Passion ensued. She stood there, lost in the tingling feelings from his kisses. Michael knew it was happening and questioned softly, "Excited?" She could only nod. Then he picked her up and deposited her on the bed. Two naked forms wrestled for hours, unable to get enough of each other. They explored each other with wet kisses, making sure not to miss one spot. Finally, in the wee hours of the evening, they fell asleep with Michael and Tess still locked in a loving embrace.

Chapter Twenty-Four: Premonition

It was two in the morning when Michael woke up in a cold sweat. His dream was more than vivid with dead FBI agents and Mansoor and his family with their throats cut. The soldier knew to trust what he was feeling from his nights alone in the jungles of Vietnam. He could sense that something wasn't right. If the jihadists could turn a U.S. senator, how hard would it be to turn an agent of the FBI? He thought to himself as he jumped out of bed and put on his jeans and a t-shirt. He pulled a light jacket from his bag and armed himself with his 380 and the 9mm luger, both with silencers. He slipped his hand into the bag again and pulled out his hunting knife. He went downstairs and jumped into a parked taxi cab. "Midtown Courtyard and fast." His tone clearly transmitted the message to the driver that this was going to be a quick trip.

It took about two minutes to get there, and Michael slipped the driver a Hamilton and was out of the cab in a flash. He went up the elevator to the 16th floor, pulled out his 380, and made his way to the rooms. He peeked around the corner to see an empty chair near the door. Okay, where's the agent? He thought.

The door to room 1615 opened, and a man came out, wiping the front of his pants, then sat in the chair in front of the room. He started to get comfortable when his head suddenly jerked to one side and blood splattered on the wall behind him. Suddenly, the door to 1615 closed. Michael thought, Why isn't he going in for the kill? He got his answer a moment later when four dark-haired men came out of room 1613. He knew from his position behind them that his shots would easily make their mark. He slowly raised his weapon and fired from the back forward. The last man dropped onto the carpeted hallway. Before the third man could react, his head was exploded. The first and second men began to react and made an effort to pull up their guns, but were too slow for a man known as The Machine, and the only sounds were bodies dropping to the floor.

The door to room 1615 opened again, and Michael shot the exposed weapon even before the man's face appeared into view. The target dropped, clutching his hand. Michael grabbed him and struck him a few times to take the fight out of him, then dragged him into the room through the still-open doorway. Once inside, he took a face cloth from the bathroom and shoved it into the man's mouth. The man struggled for only a moment as Michael began punching him until there was no reactionary response. The Machine took a towel and cut it into long three-inch strips. Then, they tied the man up securely, his hands behind his back and both legs together, and then placed him in a chair and tied him to it. He quickly retrieved the bodies in the hallway and brought them into the room.

Michael surmised that this was an FBI agent from the second shift because he didn't recognize him from the airport. He was definitely in on the attempted assassination. He needed answers quickly because there would most likely be a shift change in the morning. Michael wanted to know who was pulling the strings, and his biggest concern was how deep the treachery went in the organization he had loved for over thirty-two years. So, he wasted no time with small talk. Michael used his left hand to put the hunting knife just over the agent's right knee, with the tip right on the vastus medialis muscle, which is part of the muscular system that allows the knee to extend. He watched the agent's face, then used his right open hand to pound the knife into the muscle. The blade went in three inches, and Michael took his hands away, watching the man whimper in pain. He waited for the full effect to take place, leaned in, and whispered into the man's ear.

"I want to know who paid you and how many agents are involved? If you give me what I want the painful part of this will be over. If you play it tough, I can make the pain last a very long time. Do you understand?"

"Mm." The man muffled and nodded with complete understanding.

Michael wasn't lying to the agent, but something deep within his very being was beginning to make its way to the surface. He could feel it coming. His face appeared to change right before the agent's eyes. The Machine, in all his ferocity, was finding his way to Michael's conscious mind. The insurrection he was becoming aware of was taking him to the darkest part of his soul, and the agent in front of him was about to experience the full wrath of The Machine. The dark voice began to speak to the FBI traitor. "What you have done by turning your back on America cannot be excused. Therefore, you will be dealt with the same way I deal with the enemy, but you are even worse than they are." He cut away the agent's shirt and began to explain what was going to happen next. "I'm going to take the knife from your leg and carefully insert it into your abdomen just below the dermis, and then I'm going to remove a substantial portion of your skin so that your intestines are exposed."

"I'll talk, I'll talk." It could be heard through the muffled washcloth.

The Machine was almost out of control. He pulled the knife out of the agent's leg, and just before cutting into the abdomen, he stopped. The valuable information that might be gained by allowing the vermin to speak could be lost with torture. He thought to himself. Instead, the razor-sharp blade was placed back into his sheath. The agent watched in horror as his leg bled freely, and he thought that at any moment he would be filleted.

Suddenly, like a light switch being turned off, Michael was back. He stood and turned away from the man. Father, forgive me. He prayed for absolution. He turned back toward the agent. "Information."

As the washcloth was removed from his mouth. He began to sing like a canary. "The group that paid me is known as POTUS. Prosecution of the United States. It is run by international businessmen interested in a one-world government. They are convinced that eliminating the United States can accomplish their objective. They have people of importance in many high places of the government. You already found one since Senator Morrison is dead; I'm assuming that was you. I'm not in a position to know more than that, so please kill me quickly."

"Okay, but before I do, what's your contact's name?" Michael asked.

"Comely, he's higher up than me." He said.

"Thanks." He responded, then shot the agent in the head.

He looked at his watch. Not much time before the change of shift. He thought to himself. He searched the agent and pulled out his phone, wiped down the room, removing any trace that he was there. He exited the room, leaving the door slightly ajar. Once in the hallway, he called Tess. He knew she would be sleeping, so he let it ring until she picked up.

"It's me." He said.

"Why did you leave?" She asked, half asleep.

"The agency has been compromised. I just killed one of the agents guarding Mansoor and four jihadists. They were there to kill them all."

"What…what? Where are you?" she asked, quickly waking to full consciousness.

"I'll need your car. I'm going to get Mansoor and his family gone before the change of shift. Throw my stuff together, and I'll call you once I have them secure. Trust no one, Tess, especially a guy named Comely. I'll fill in all the details then. I love you."

He ended the call and made his way to Mansoor's room. He knocked gently two or three times. Mansoor looked through the peephole. Seeing his boss, he quickly opened the door and said, "I heard noises. Is everything alright?"

"Get the family together. We need to get out of here now." Michael said firmly.

"Okay, boss," Mansoor said, then left the door open and got his family and their belongings secured.

"Good morning, everyone, we're going to go for a little trip," Michael said with a smile to remove the sense of danger. Mansoor used the same tone to translate into Persian. They made their way down the hall to the stairs. Michael led the way down two flights and then across the hallway to the service elevator. It read Employees Only. Once inside, he pressed the ground floor, which was the floor below the lobby, where the laundry machines were, and he escorted them past the night shift employees who were too busy washing towels and sheets to even notice them making their way to the stairs that led up to the alley.

“Wait here!” Michael said and made his way to the front of the hotel to grab a cab. He took out the agent’s phone and sent a text message to Comely. It read, All the death was caused by Firestorm.

A few minutes later, a cab appeared in the alley. The cab driver and Michael got out, grabbed the luggage, and threw it into the trunk. The family got into the backseat of the car. Michael got into the front seat. “Drive.” He said with authority.

Chapter Twenty-Five: Refuge

The taxi pulled up to the curb in front of the Fairfield Inn. Michael gave the cab driver twenty dollars after he removed their luggage. The valet already had Tess's car up front with the door open. "Mr. Devlin, your wife said to drive safely, and your suitcase is in the trunk already."

"Thanks, kid." Michael got a ten out of his wallet and handed it to him. Mansoor helped put the suitcases in the trunk, and they all got in. Michael got behind the wheel and made his way to the 78 west.

"Everyone rest, this is going to take a while," Michael said once they were on the expressway.

"Where are we going, boss?" Mansoor asked quietly.

"I'm taking you to my home in Pennsylvania. No one will find you there." Michael said confidently.

"The people I worked for are like an octopus with tentacles that are very far-reaching. I hope you are right." Mansoor warned.

"I made you a promise, and my word is my bond. Try and get some sleep now." He told his informant.

Michael prayed hard during the almost four-hour drive to Gettysburg. He asked God to spare the family in his charge, to give him the strength to forge ahead despite the danger looming over his very existence. He only stopped once for gas and paid in cash. He would leave no clues if at all possible. He stopped for donuts at a Krispy Kreme drive-through just as the sun was rising.

Michael was looking at his old town and the beautiful snow that gently covered the ground. He was glad he missed the storm but thrilled that God left a magnificent blanket of white. He wondered if the little boys in the back seat of the car had ever seen snow. When he parked the car in his garage, the family began to wake up.

"Good morning," Michael said lyrically to lighten the mood. "Let's get you inside so you can get settled. The place is probably a bit dusty. Nobody has been here for quite some time." Mansoor translated Michael's words to his wife.

Adiva rolled up her sleeves and looked under the kitchen sink for cleaning supplies, found a plastic bucket, some wash rags, and some all-purpose cleaner. She filled the bucket with soapy water and began cleaning off all the counters and the kitchen table. Michael and Mansoor got the luggage, and the twins went to the window to look at the winter wonderland outside. Michael cleared off the dusty dining room table and placed the box of donuts on it. He watched as Adiva sat the boys down, said a prayer of thanks with them, and placed a wonderful powdered sugar crème-filled donut in front of each. In seconds, their cheeks were covered with the confectioner's delight.

Michael put Mansoor and Adiva's luggage in Joshua's old room. His wife, Elizabeth, made it into a beautiful guest room after Josh moved out. He remembered that there were clean white towels in the top drawer of the dresser, took them out, and placed them on the bed. He looked around the room and noticed the curtains Elle had made to match the quilted bedspread. She was so excited when she finished, and Michael was sorry he didn't make a bigger deal about it.

Elle used to tell Michael that when Josh had children, they would need a room of their own. So, the other bedroom was decorated with Disney pictures on the wall and a daybed with a trundle bed underneath. She even saved Joshua's toys and stuffed animals in a wooden toy box Michael made when their son was very young. He put the twins' suitcases just inside the room so Adiva could take care of them.

His face began to get flushed as a lifetime of memories began to come to the surface. He felt like Elle was going to come up behind him and wrap her arms around his waist. This was his refuge from the horrors in Washington, D.C. The place he loved to come home to before she got so very sick. His mind couldn't escape those bad memories when she suffered through the cancer chemotherapy treatments that ravaged her body.

He went back into the living room with evidence that Adiva had been there already. He went to the old record player, and there was Neil Diamond's September Morn. He never put it away after their anniversary dance that September 10th in 2001. He wondered if Elle listened to it on occasion while he was driving back and forth from D.C. He would love to dance with her in his arms one more time. His memory played back those precious moments as he just stood there against the wall, staring at the living room rug.

Mansoor tapped him on the shoulder, and it brought him back to the present. Michael asked his guest if he needed anything. Mansoor asked what he could do to help.

"I'm glad you asked, because if we don't get busy, your wife will be finished. I'll get the vacuum cleaner out and put on the tube attachment to get the dust off the curtains, and then you can vacuum the floors, okay?"

Mansoor watched the boys as they quietly made their way through their second crème-filled donut and kept them occupied while Adiva was almost finished with dusting the furniture and cleaning all the counters in the house. When Michael finished the drapes, he gave the vacuum to his guest.

"It's all yours, my friend. I'm going to go shopping in town for food. So, is there anything special your wife likes?"

"She likes chocolate very much," Mansoor answered with a wink.

"Okay, I'll be gone for an hour or so." Michael left the house, took two steps, and went back in. Mansoor was already attacking the floors. Michael went into his room and came out a moment later with the 9 mm, tapped Mansoor on the shoulder, and had him watch as he put the weapon on top of the dining room hutch.

"Just in case," Michael said and was gone again.

Michael made his way to Harrisburg Road and the Weis Market. It had been quite some time since Michael went shopping for groceries. He was wondering what to buy and opted to buy almost everything. When he got to the checkout, his cart was full to the top. The cashier watched as he began to unload all the food products on the revolving counter.

She smiled at him and finally said, "Hungry, Hon?"

Michael answered, "Just stocking up."

She was scanning the last few items when Michael remembered the chocolate. Behind him in the check-out lane were bars of dark chocolate, milk chocolate, even cookies and crème chocolate bars. He scooped up four of each kind and put them up for her to scan.

The cashier was getting a kick out of a man who really didn't look like he knew what he was doing.

The bill was three hundred forty-five dollars and thirty-nine cents. He removed his wallet and took out four hundred-dollar bills. The cashier took out a pen and marked each bill to ensure it was real. He wanted to tell her that he just printed those, so be careful, but decided against it. He put all the groceries in the car and made his way home. He called Tess on the way.

"Hello sweetheart, first off, we're safe." He told her.

"I'm glad to hear that because all hell is breaking loose here." She said emphatically.

"Fill me in." He said, concerned.

"The agency is doing an internal investigation. The DOJ is checking bank accounts, and everyone is under suspicion. We've been able to sidestep the press, but you know how long that will last. We've got more leaks than an old faucet."

"Roger that," Michael interjected.

"Ted didn't come to New York. I called him last night after you left and told him that I think the same group that saved your informant overseas pulled him out of the hotel. I told him they must have been keeping an eye on him because they took out the terrorists and apparently tortured the agent for information. They're running prints on the weapons discovered at the scene. Is there anything I should know?" She asked, hoping for clarification, that he didn't leave his prints behind.

"The agent at the door was shot by the one slightly tortured. I shot the weapon from his hand before taking out the terrorists. I cleaned up after myself. So, I don't expect they'll find my prints anywhere. The story you told Hobson sounds plausible. Let's give him a bit more to chew on. Tell him you were contacted this morning with more information about what's going on. The group wanting to take out Mansoor is called POTUS, Prosecution of the United States."

"You've got to be kidding," Tess said, surprised.

"The agent told me that the ultimate goal is to destroy America and establish a world government. It's apparently being run by some big-time business moguls from different countries, and they're using the jihadists as puppets to do all the dirty work. Pretty arrogant if you ask me." Michael editorialized.

"God help us," Tess exclaimed.

"That's probably a good prayer. Tell your boss the name of the group that's in the middle of all this and took out the senator is called Firestorm. Tell him they uncovered the whole thing in Galveston when they discovered there was a plot to kill the President. Maybe that can take some of the heat off me." Michael said hopefully.

"Yes, that's a great lie. My gosh, you're really good at being deceitful." She informed him.

"Thanks, honey. By the way, I just spent over three hundred dollars at the grocery store." Michael told her.

"Where are you?" She asked.

"That's better left unsaid for now. When you find out who the bad guys are, we can get this family settled." He paused for a moment. "As a matter of fact, the more information about all this in the press might remove any further attempts to kill them. Mansoor's information is very limited, so he can't be much of a threat since he was only involved with the jihadists. Aqeel was higher up the food chain, and he's the one who led us to Kahn." Michael waited for her input.

"You're right. This could work. The more they're exposed, the harder it will be for their plan to succeed." Tess concurred.

Then she changed the subject and asked, "Why did you buy so much food?"

"Well, it all looked so good, and there's such a variety. I ended up buying four of everything." He said, justifying his actions.

"You're a nut, and I've got to go. Watch the news tonight and tomorrow for how the press handles this. Love you." Tess hung up before he could tell her back.

He pulled up the driveway and into the garage. Mansoor came out and, seeing Michael juggle with the bags, helped him carry all the food into the house. Inside, Adiva was wiping down the inside of the empty refrigerator. She went right for the bags and took out all the products that needed to be in the freezer. The cupboards were bare, so she began organizing. Four kinds of cereal, four kinds of yogurt, four kinds of prepared tomato sauce, and all the bags contained quite a variety of products. Michael made sure to include plenty of vegetables that he knew were used in Middle Eastern meals.

Adiva asked her husband in Persian with a smile, "He can't seem to make up his mind, can he? He bought too much of everything."

Michael came in as she finished and asked Mansoor what she said. Mansoor told him, "She says you are a great shopper." Then he told his wife in Persian what he told Michael.

"Merci…Thank you." Michael said in two languages, hoping she would understand.

She responded in English, with a big grin, "You are welcome."

With the house clean, Mansoor took the boys outside to play in the snow. Michael watched at first, then went out to teach the boys how to build a snowman. Once the form was made, Michael ran into the mudroom where Elle kept an old top hat filled with eight black stones, a corn cob pipe, and a bright red scarf. They decorated the blank form and, in minutes, brought Frosty the snowman to life.

Later that night they sat down for dinner together. Adiva prepared a wonderful meal, and Michael said, "Let's say a prayer of thanks. With that, he put out his hands, and all at the table did the same. Michael said, "Lord, we come to this wonderful meal and give thanks for such bounty, but more we thank you for your great sacrifice to make us part of your family. We ask that you be with us in the days ahead. We ask this through your son, our Lord Jesus Christ. Amen.

They watched Michael waiting for him to start eating. He looked at them and realized what was happening. He said, "Eat well." He picked up the cooked vegetables, took some, and passed them to Adiva. They all smiled and began to eat. Michael looked around the table and smiled. A long time had passed since his house was a home, and this night it was a home again.

Once his guests were asleep, Michael turned on CNN to see what they were reporting after the press got information from the hotel manager and Tess's leak. He couldn't believe what anchor Jefferson Kooper was reporting. "Last night, six men were killed in a shootout at the Courtyard in downtown New York. No details available at this time. We will keep you informed."

Michael thought to himself, That's it! Are you kidding me? He picked up his cell phone and called Tess.

"What happened?" He asked abruptly.

"I don't know. They certainly had enough to do a more comprehensive report. They didn't even mention that two FBI agents were killed." She replied.

"Something stinks. Who's in charge at CNN?" Michael asked.

"Let me check really quickly. Hang on, it's coming up on my computer. It says Jim Reardon is the current CEO with a net worth of over thirty billion dollars." Tess informed her husband.

"Well, I guess if he doesn't want something aired, it doesn't get in the news." He commented to her.

"Give it a few days. If another station starts giving the story attention, the others will have to, too." She told him hopefully.

"Okay. One more thing, if we wanted to get Mansoor into a witness protection program, could you talk with Director Reyes of the Marshall Service without too many people knowing?" He asked.

"I'll give him a call and give him a hypothetical scenario and see how he responds. If he gives me useful information, it might be a great next step." Tess assured him.

"Okay. That's good. As far as the news report, at least it's out there, and whoever is sending out assassins might not want to make any more attempts for fear of getting exposed, especially to take out an ex-low-level jihadist. In the meantime, I'll just be here for now. I'm missing you, my wife." Michael confessed.

“Me too. I will keep you informed on our investigation. It's late, babe. Try to get some well-deserved sleep. I know for you it isn’t very often. I love you.” Tess told him.

“Love you back, kid.” He said before hanging up.

She’s right, a good night’s sleep in my own bed is just what the doctor ordered. He told himself.

Michael slid under the sheets with his 380 under the pillow. He lay there looking at the ceiling. He asked God to watch over him and keep everyone in his house safe. His eyes closed, and he was out.

Chapter Twenty-Six: Complicit

Sitting in his beautifully decorated office with a view of the Eiffel Tower, Naqeem Kahn picked up his phone and contacted Jim Reardon. A moment later, the voice on the other end said clearly, "Kahn, it would appear there is a fly in the ointment."

The Middle Eastern businessman was unfamiliar with the idiom, so he inquired about the meaning. The response was, "We have ourselves a problem, and he is pretty pissed off. I have a source at the FBI, and he says a group calling themselves Firestorm is the one attempting to mess up our plan. It would appear your jihadist comrades aren't as good as we anticipated. It has been one mistake after another."

"I know." He said with a bit of indignation in his voice. He quickly tempered his anger. "I have been watching the news, and you're right, it is a problem. What does Rosor want us to do?" Kahn asked with concern.

"He said he was told that we are to take care of it. His focus has been to work with college professors all around the U.S. to promote his worldview and one world government, and he's been pretty successful in having them demonize anyone who tries to speak on Nationalism or conservative issues." Reardon explained.

"Yes, but without another major catastrophe as a catalyst, we will be hard-pressed to promote our agenda," Kahn responded.

"That's exactly right. The other members of POTUS are willing to fund any endeavor that we come up with so put on your thinking cap and let's get something going. Stay off the internet because this crazy Firestorm group is getting too much intelligence on our plans. He has indicated he's going to send his specialists to resolve the Firestorm problem. By the way, how much does this Amoli character know about us?" Reardon asked.

"He was middle management and was not privy to any information about our group. He oversaw the jihadists that were massacred by Firestorm, but I don't like loose ends, and Gabany thought he might have turned, which is why I had a team go to eliminate him. He must have been watched by that group since they helped him escape from Tehran." Kahn explained.

Reardon thought for a moment and then said, "If he doesn't know anything, he's no longer a threat to us. So, forget him and let's move forward. Since you've already tried to have them killed, that Firestorm group will devote a lot of time to continuing to protect him, and that means they'll be preoccupied. Agreed?"

"Yes, that is a very good idea. I'll get back to you soon." Kahn said and hung up the phone.

***

Chet Avery saw Ted Hobson as a great replacement for Angelino, but mostly wanted to keep an eye on him, since Avery had a proclivity for sex with children and believed in Machiavelli's quote of keeping your friends close and your enemies even closer. Hobson's history working against human trafficking meant that he knew a lot about that particular subject, and that worried Chet.

Ted Hobson was very busy getting oriented as deputy director of the FBI after the untimely death of Chet Avery. He had moved up the chain of command quickly and was sure that much of his work in conjunction with Interpol was the reason for his rapid advancement. His part in arresting an international group of human traffickers, who were abducting children for sex slaves in New York, Europe, the Philippines, and South America, brought him great praise from his superiors. Ted worked as part of a team that included Jacques Dubois, and over time, the two became good friends.

Ted was arranging his new office when the phone rang. He picked up the receiver to hear, "Bonjour mon ami (hello my friend)."

"Jacques, I didn't expect to hear from you already. It's only been a few days," Ted said, excited to hear from him.

"You made it sound important. So, I told my superiors I was going to Paris to see my girlfriend. I flew there and went to the office of Kahn, pretending to be interested in doing business with him, and while I was there, I placed a transmitter under his desk. The call that came today was very interesting. However, you can't make out what was being said on the other end. I thought perhaps your tech team could enhance the other voice. Kahn's words were very clear and may help you in your investigation. I have taken the recording, and I am sending it to you as an email attachment." Jacques said in his best English.

"Thanks, Jacques," Ted responded.

He went to his email, pulled up the message, and played it a few times, taking notes. His friend was right; the other voice was inaudible, but finding out about a group called Firestorm that was involved in getting the informant out of Iran was huge. He thought to himself, What is their group? Who was on the phone, and what does Rosor, the business magnate, political activist, and philanthropist, have to do with it? Most important is what is their agenda?

Ted called the head of the science and technology branch of the FBI (STB), Barbara Heller. He got her voice mail and left her a message to call him ASAP. His next call was to Tess Lamia, as head of the terrorist task force; her input would be invaluable.

Tess answered her cell immediately. "Hey Ted, I'm glad you called. I have more information for you." She didn't give him a chance to speak. "I found out the name of the group that apparently has been involved since the killings in Galveston."

"You mean Firestorm." Ted interrupted her.

"How did you know that?" She asked very suspiciously.

"My contact in France was able to plant a bug in Kahn's office, and I picked up some information from a call, but all I could get was one side of the conversation. I'm going to have the STB try to enhance the audio to pick up the other voice. Who contacted you?" Ted asked.

"One of the members of Firestorm called me less than an hour ago. I don't know how they got my number, but they said what's been going on has been the work of an organization called POTUS, which stands for prosecution of the United States. I know Kahn is involved and possibly Jim Reardon." She informed her boss.

"I think we can add George Rosor. What's their game?" Ted asked.

"A one-world government controlled by the people who have the most money. It's unbelievable, Ted." She said it, but was having trouble conceiving that it was a real possibility.

"Okay, Tess, don't tell anybody what we've discussed. I don't know who we can trust. If what you just told me is true, then this

POTUS can buy off anyone, and it would appear the only help we're going to get is from this mysterious group called Firestorm. God help us!" he said, expressing his feeling of hopelessness.

Tess called Michael to fill him in. The two discussed continuing to keep the family in hiding until such time as it would be safe to get them into a witness protection program, if it were even possible. Once the business part of their conversation was over. He told her he loved her. She responded in kind.

"I want you to come out for a visit. Is it safe?" he asked her.

"I can get away for a few days as long as I can be available by phone in case Ted needs me for something. Are you going to tell me where you are?" she asked coyly.

Michael picked up on it and told her she was getting him excited. She giggled. "We sure don't get to do a lot of that, do we?" he asked her.

"What do you mean?" She queried.

"Laugh and just be happy." He answered her.

"Where are you?" She asked again.

"Just get on the 78 west. Oh, wait a minute…you don't have a car." Michael said with a slight laugh.

"Oh, you're asking for it, buster." She said, pretending to be angry.

"If you know you're not being tailed, come to Gettysburg. I'll text you the address. Now get moving." He said as an order.

"Yes, sir." She said with another giggle and hung up.

Tess had a great idea. She got dressed and had a taxi take her to a Honda dealership where she bought a top-of-the-line Odyssey. The mini-van was fully equipped with leather seats, an awesome sound system, and all the bells and whistles. It was a beautiful silver color that she thought would match Michael's hair, and she told herself not to forget to tell him that. She was sure that would get them into a wrestling match.

She drove the vehicle home and filled her overnight bag with a few essentials. She checked the weather on her phone and brought her winter coat and gloves. Within an hour, she was on the road and heading west.

She went to her contact list and pulled up the name Xavier Sanchez. Her cell phone made contact after just one ring.

"X S?" She asked the voice on the other end.

"Ms. Lamia, if you're calling me, I'm guessing my friend is in trouble again," Xavier said as a matter of fact.

"He's always in trouble. You've been keeping track of him by the news reports, haven't you?"

"Pretty good for an old man." He answered back.

"Are you still doing work on cars?"

"On and off, when I feel like it." He answered.

"Michael needs some adjustments made for his new van. Do you know what I mean?" She asked, already knowing that he knew what she was talking about.

"Yes, that can be arranged." He said. "You want a War Wagon."

"Absolutely." She said.

“When?” He asked her.

“I’ll let you know. So, try and stay out of jail, okay?” She asked more like a command.

“What kind of car is it?”

“New Honda Odyssey.” She answered.

“I’ll start ordering parts.”

“Okay. Be discreet and thanks, Xavier.” She said with appreciation.

A moment later, her phone beeped a message, and there was the address in Gettysburg. She put it into her GPS, put on some great driving music, and thought about the man she loved. It was going to be a four-hour drive, and she was in her second hour when the phone rang. It was Ted.

“Hey Ted, what’s the latest?” she asked.

“I just got a call from Barbara Heller at STB, and she was able to enhance the caller’s voice. I’ll play it for you.” Ted told her, then played the conversation.

“Wow, their arrogance makes me sick. Okay, Ted, send it to me as an attachment, and if that Firestorm group contacts me again, I’ll play it for them. I hate that they're confusing our college kids. I’ve been hearing that conservative speakers weren’t being allowed to speak. Now we know why.” She told him. “By the way Ted, my husband and I are going to spend a few days together before he is gone again. If you need me to call, but I’ll be out of town for at least a few days, maybe a week. I’ll see where we are on all this and if your French friend gets any more information, especially if he can come up with more names involved, let me know, okay?” she asked.

"Great, take a few days, and when you get back, we need to strategize what and how we're going to deal with this, because we don't know who to trust." He said, frustrated.

"Okay, Ted, thanks for the time off. I think David and I really need it. He's been gone too long." Tess tapped the phone off.

She continued to focus on the road, but her mind was questioning her decision. How can you afford to take a few days off? Tess almost turned the van around, but she needed to see him to know that he was alright, to kiss her husband one more time.

Chapter Twenty-Seven: Repose

The beautiful winter day was coming to an end with just enough afternoon sunlight to make the alabaster snow sparkle. The twins were given two round metal disks and just enough hill to keep them occupied for hours. Adiva was busy cooking in the kitchen and was able to watch her children frolic joyfully in the snow. Mansoor and Michael were busy working on the fifty-five Chevy Michael had stored in his garage. It was a project he thought he and Joshua would work on together, but never had the chance after 9/11.

"You're pretty good with a wench, Mansoor. When did you learn how to work on cars?" Michael asked with a smile.

"Before I was radicalized." He responded and then added, "That was so very long ago."

"A lifetime for me, too. I never thought I would be a warrior fighting for his country again." Michael admitted.

"You were a soldier?" Mansoor asked.

"Vietnam," Michael answered, then changed the subject. "Pass me a crescent wrench."

Mansoor understood it wasn't something to probe further. The men went back to being just two guys working on a beautiful old car. Michael looked down at his watch. He thought she should be here soon. "I'll be right back." He told Mansoor, wiped the grease off his hands, and walked down the wet driveway.

As he reached the mailbox, he saw a new van turn the corner. He looked closely, and suddenly he felt butterflies in his stomach. It was Tess. She pulled into the driveway and rolled down the window. "Need a ride, soldier?"

"Nice wheels." He said, admiring the vehicle.

"I bought it for you," She said with a smile. Michael's mouth opened in complete surprise. "I'm gonna need my car back."

Michael moved closer to her window and kissed her softly. "This is a hell of a gift, and it isn't even my birthday."

"You'll need to make a trip to San Antonio soon…for alterations."

"X S?" Michael asked.

"He's already ordering the parts." She answered.

Michael smiled and then got into the passenger seat. Once inside, he kissed her again. Her heart was so full of love, but she was now at the home of Elizabeth, and she was feeling a bit insecure. Michael could sense something was wrong and picked up on it quickly.

"Tess, Elle knew you had feelings for me before I ever did." He admitted to her.

"How do you know that?" She asked.

"She used to say things like, you know, Tess has feelings for you, and I would say no, we're just a good team. Then she would roll her eyes at me like I was an idiot, and I was, because I had no idea you did…not really. So, I think she'd be happy we found each other." He explained to her.

"Really?" She asked.

"Yes…really." He told her and kissed her again to put an exclamation point on the conversation.

One kiss turned into ten, until Tess broke it off and told him about the bugged phone call. Michael listened intently. When he finished, he told Tess, "It sounds like I will be dealing with assassins. I wonder who HE is? At least our family is in there, may have a life after all. Can you give them new identities?"

"I'm going to walk it through myself. I've made some friends in the U. S. Marshall's office, but I'll be checking all the financials before I move forward." She told him.

"Okay, let's get you better acquainted with the family," Michael said.

The two drove down the driveway and parked near the garage. Mansoor was still working on the Chevy but recognized Tess and waved his greasy hand "hello" as she exited the van.

Michael went into the garage, grabbed a work rag, and threw it at Mansoor. "Let's go talk with your wife."

The three entered the house, and Mansoor told his wife to join them. Over the next hour, Tess explained to the couple what would happen next. She told them about getting new identities, and they would have all the appropriate documents, like birth certificates for all, and a marriage license. They would receive an allowance from the government, a car, and be relocated somewhere in the United States.

"We have to change our names?" Mansoor asked because he was concerned that his children might be confused.

"Just your last name, but you can keep the same initials. I think your boys will be able to learn a new last name, and it will become easier for them once they start school." Tess explained to help reduce the stressfulness of the situation.

Tess went on to explain. "You'll need to learn our driving laws as soon as possible and take a driver's test for a license. In our country, this can also be another form of identification. You will also be assigned a supervisor who will be watching over you to ensure your safety. This will be someone I vet myself, so he is someone you'll be able to trust."

"What about work?" Mansoor asked, this time looking at Michael.

"Well, you're very good with a wrench, and you seem to know a lot about cars. What about going to some classes to get a mechanics certificate? Tess's people will even help you find a job, and there's no rush because the government stipend is roughly sixty thousand a year." Mansoor nodded as Adiva held his arm.

"It's a very good start, but in America, the sky is the limit on how much you can earn. Auto mechanics earn between thirty-five and forty-five thousand dollars a year. So, you should be able to have a pretty good life here. The best part is you can practice your faith without fear of persecution." Michael said with a smile.

Mansoor told them it sounded like a great plan and asked, "When does this all happen?"

He looked at Michael, and Michael turned to Tess, who said, "This is going to happen in about three weeks. I'll start making the calls necessary to get the ball rolling, and I'll hand-pick your supervisor when I return to Washington, D.C. Michael will stay here with you until we're ready for the move."

Adiva spoke to her husband in their home language quietly. "My wife just said to tell both of you, thank you with all our hearts." Michael looked at them both and said, "Your work saved thousands of lives, but now it is done, my friend."

That night, after the family went to bed, Michael reclined on his bed with his shirt off, staring at the bathroom door. He wondered what was taking Tess so long. Then the door opened slowly, and Tess came out in a cute blue nightie. She looked almost afraid as she approached the bed, very insecure about being in the home he shared with his wife. Michael picked up on her insecurity instantly and moved to the edge of the bed, took his hands, wrapped them around her uncovered thighs, and kissed her belly through the lacy material. He looked up at her and smiled. She met his eyes and began to relax a little. He slowly lifted the nightie to reveal she wasn't wearing panties and gave out a soft moan.

His desire was to hold her and make her feel better about where they were, but his passion took over, and his mouth moved over her soft, fragrant skin. His kisses were wet and his lips so hot that she felt on fire. Then he stood up, and she used her fingers to remove the buttons of his Levi's. She giggled with surprise as his pants slipped to the floor, and her wide-eyed look made him laugh when she noticed he was naked. He was very careful to be extra gentle with her as they moved together as one. Their movement was slow and rhythmic as the two lovers met each other halfway. They stared at each other as Michael put his hands on each side of her shoulders so he could watch her as they both shuddered together. Their breathing became a unified gasp of satisfaction. They resisted making too much noise, and that seemed to intensify the moment through their restraint. Afterwards, they remained together for some time, and Michael continued to stare at her and she at him. They were speaking volumes of love without a word spoken. Their eyes began to tear, then Michael dropped his chest to hers and whispered in her ear, “I love you.” Tess began to cry, overwhelmed with love for her husband and truly feeling his love for her, something she was learning to appreciate with every passing moment.

Epilogue

Michael couldn't remember when he last had a whole week to just be a man in love. He took the time to give Tess a tour of the area where he grew up. He also couldn't resist telling her many of the stories he heard about the ghosts of Gettysburg, which she refused to believe. They took long walks in the evening, holding hands and acting like it was their first love. However, the week ended much too quickly for both of them.

Tess kissed her husband a hundred times before leaving for Washington in her car and spent the first two hours crying and wiping the tears from her eyes, partially joyous over the amazing time they had together and sad not knowing when or if she would ever see him again.

Tess had set the wheels in motion for the witness protection program. She was feeling good about the fact that this group of fanatics who wanted to rule the world had lost interest in the family she got to know during her trip. Her mind kept returning to the reference of some unknown group going after Firestorm, and who was the he that was mentioned? She wasn't sure how much to trust Ted, but all indications were that he might very well be one of the good guys.

Two weeks later, a U.S. Marshall by the name of Elliot Thompson arrived at the house in Gettysburg to find a family of four. Michael was parked far enough away not to be seen but close enough to see what was happening. Tess had called to let him know that it was happening and didn't want him to be seen by anyone from the government. Once they were whisked away, Michael made his way to the traffic circle in the heart of town, glancing momentarily at the statue of Abraham Lincoln with his stove top hat in his hand. He wondered if the American president was given the gift of prophecy regarding the demise of the republic. He shook it off and drove onto Baltimore Street. Once he got on Interstate 81, he settled in for a very long twenty-four-hour drive.

Michael took the time to have a conversation with God. He thanked Him for his protection and for keeping Mansoor and his family safe. "Lord, the road ahead doesn't look any better than the ones we traveled up to this point but I will trust in you to do what is in your plan. If I am going to be with you soon, thank you for allowing me to know a great love again, however brief. If I am to continue, watch over me, but more importantly, continue to bless this country in spite of all its imperfections. It is our human nature that keeps us from you, as the temptations here on earth are sometimes very hard to resist. Please forgive me of all my sins. Through your sacrifice on the cross, I am saved from the hell I most assuredly deserve. I love you, Abba."

***

Hiroshi Nakamura was visibly upset upon seeing the news report about the assassination of Grady Morrison. He had invested heavily in the development of a key resource for his group's plan of global unification. "The United States needs to pay for the death of my grandfather on that horrific day of August 6th, 1945, with the bombing of Hiroshima, and revenge will be mine."

Philip N. Rogone